JOJO

PART ONE

A Novel by

C-LOVE

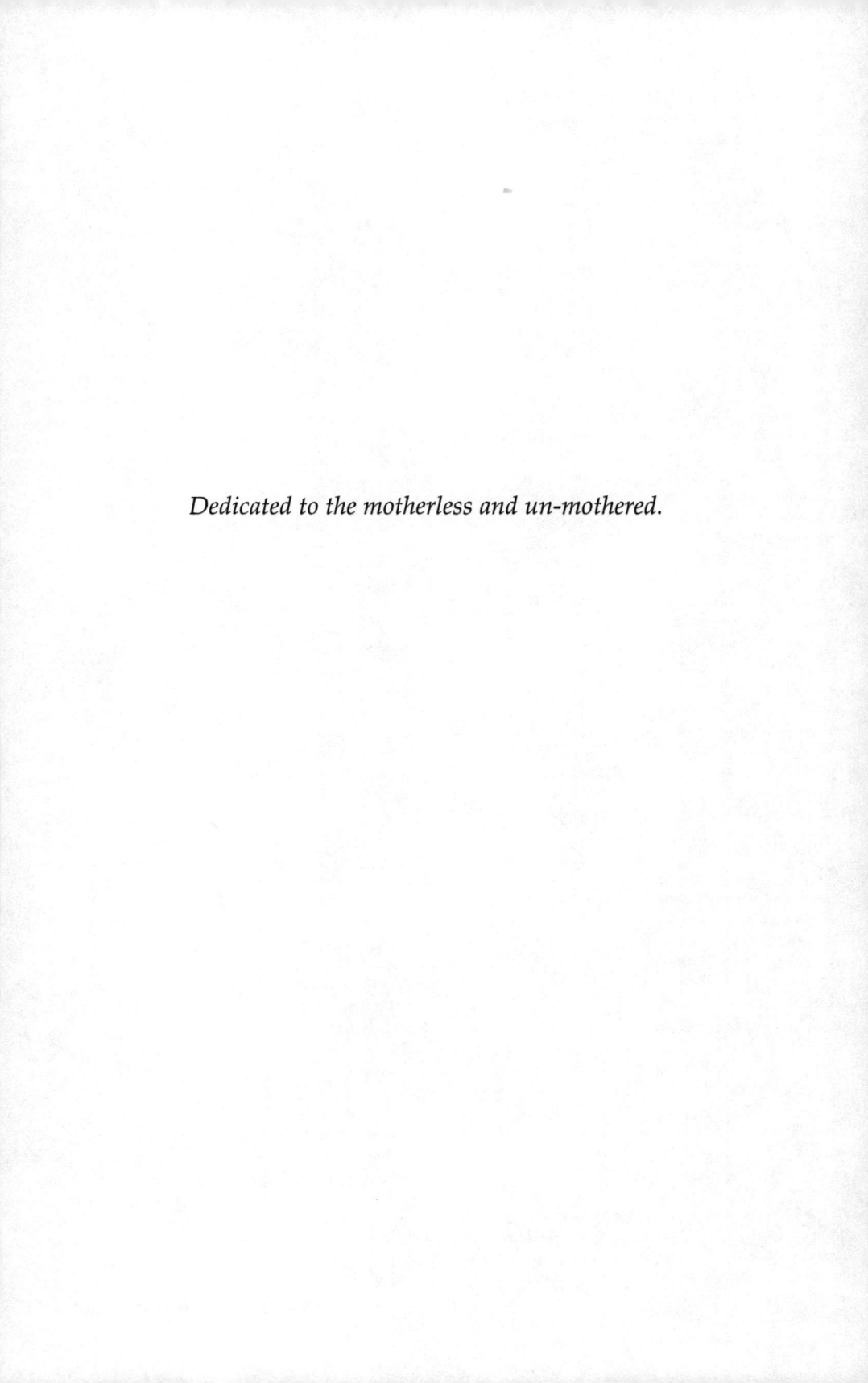

Dedicated to the motherless and un-mothered.

PROLOGUE

22 JUN 1973—
HAZOU COUNTY, VA

*I*t was a muggy night at the backwoods compound. The atmosphere smelled of recent rain. A canopy of bright stars dotted the pitch black sky. Wind blew through the branches as owls, nocturnal insects, and rustling leaves masked the looming tension. One and all, hurried to be front and center. The baby Abba Yisrael divined would soon arrive.

Within thirty minutes of the summons, the seventy plus-year old Haitian midwife and her assistant, accessed the main house via a side door. A pungent blend of patchouli and myrrh wafted through the air. The older woman gripped the younger for support, while traversing a narrow corridor, and small set of stairs.

As they entered a bedchamber, Shiphrah greeted the occupants. "Shalom (*Hello*)." After unpacking her time-worn bag, she examined her reclined charge.

"Nana—I'm so glad you're here. The pain is unbearable. I don't know how much longer I can take this."

"Stop your foolishness, child. You'll bear and live much like the two thousand or so women I assisted before you." She dried her hands and brushed the hair plastered to Yasmine's face. "Both of you are doing fine."

"*Oooooh*, there's another."

"Relax and breathe deeply, as we practiced."

Yasmine stared into the elder's glittering gem-like orbs, and felt relief. The pregnancy hadn't been easy. Long white

1

strands twisted round her crown, forming a halo. The hymn she hummed, soothed like a cool breeze.

"Get some rest. The wee one will alert us when she's ready."

Yasmine slept for the first time in hours.

"Throw open a window! It's hot as Hades in here. No wonder her gown's drenched."

Aaliyah stepped forward. "I think it's best we remove it. I'll find dry sheets and blankets then get her resettled."

"Your plan is sound. This may take a while."

Her newest assistant was the most competent doula Shiphrah ever trained. She was at peace having found a suitable replacement. Her days of running from county to county were over. This would be her last labor and delivery.

Around midnight, Yasmine startled everyone, awakening in a panic. "Oh...*oh*...*oh*...here comes another one! The worst yet."

"Aaliyah, please prepare the table. Send that meddlesome scamp on the other side of the door to get us some towels and boiling water. When you're finished, get my rubbing oils then use the lemon juice in the blue bottle to cleanse yourself. I have my own."

While the waiting continued, Aaliyah wiped sweat from Yasmine's brow. The anxious expectant father sat in the adjacent building listening to his love's guttural moans. As the contractions grew longer, stronger and closer together, the birthers toiled to keep her comfortable. Before long, she howled a desire to push.

Shiphrah limped to her side. "I'm here! Are you ready, dear?"

"I'm scared, but yes, I think so," whimpered Yasmine between winces. "*Owww!* Please, get this baby out of me, or let me die."

"Aaliyah–the hour, we've waited for, is here. She's small, so let's see if you and I, can get her into the chair, ourselves. Take my hand, child. Let's stand." The older woman was much stronger than she appeared.

Once Yasmine was in the correct position, Shiphrah checked her cervix. Yasmine groaned as her pelvis muscles tightened.

"I have wonderful news—you're fully dilated." She took

Yasmine's finger and positioned it on top of the emerging head.

"Oh my."

"When you feel the pain rise again, breathe in then push it out as hard as you can."

"Okay…its time."

"Now push…push, Beloved! *Ahhhh* yes, you're doing fine…. the baby's crowning….Ye are mighty." She snapped at the observant woman assembled. "Pray sisters!"

A sanguine chorus crooned in unison:

"Baruch Atah Adonai Eloheinu Melech Ha-olam shehecheyanu vi-kimanu vi-higiyanu la-z'man ha-zeh"

(*Blessed are You, oh Lord, our God, King of the universe, who has allowed us to live, has preserved us, and has enabled us to reach this season*).

After the third recitation of the sacred invocation, the instinctive urge of bearing down came over Yasmine again.

Shiphrah coached in a heavily accented voice. "Now, push with all of ye might. Yes…Give honor and glory to Yahweh for this day. Good…good...the shoulders are out…..one more…a big one and you're done."

With all the strength in her body, Yasmine performed as described. Shiphrah breathed a sigh of relief when the legs were free. A few seconds later—"Waaaaaah! Waaaaah! Wahhhhh!"

"Se yon ti fi! (*It's a girl*) Bondye bon. (*God is good*)"

Thunderous applause erupted with the newest member of the tribe's first cry. "A veil. Beautiful, tibebe (*little baby*). Unique, agile and strong." She marveled, while inspecting the newborn for imperfections.

The caul (extra skin) was removed, and placed in a jar. Her delicate incisions on both sides of the baby's face ensured there'd only be faint marks. Next, she was put on her beaming mother's chest, and covered with a blanket. The amniotic sac, sitting in a bowl, and umbilical cord were left attached.

"Nana, should we cut it, now?"

"Patience. Nature dictates when. The tibebe reabsorbs the

blood then we'll tie it off. Some mums plant a bush or sapling where they bury the pouch. I've even heard of a few eating it." She giggled, finding her pupil's shock amusing.

With the transfer complete, she placed the infant in a basin of water, enriched with flowers petals, herbs, and essential oils. Shiphrah cleaned her nostrils and ears, then rinsed her bushy cap. After drying and swaddling her, they handed the baby off to her doting father. Ten minutes later, the midwives had packed, and departed.

At the naming ceremony held the following evening, Abba Yisrael explained the choice and significance of Joanna (*God is gracious*).

Yasmine, seated on an elevated throne, beamed with pride as the crowd offered prayers for the princess' health and good fortune. Calling her happy would've been an understatement.

Women served a vegan feast as children danced for the circle of men draped in vibrant robes adorned with gilded regalia. Revelrous praise and worship songs filled, even the dark-hearted souls in the mix, with glee.

The birth of *"little star"* changed her perspective. Instead of seeking external acceptance, she focused on her *"present."*

She'd prayed for clarity, and God gave her a daughter.

Yasmine was heavy with her second child, when she began bleeding. The midwife was called two days later to assess her needs. Appalled by the lack of concern for the infirmed, Aaliyah demanded Abba Yisrael's attention.

After driving until dawn, he arrived to find his wife unresponsive. He knelt by her bedside, and placed his head on her stomach.

"Yasmine is ill. Both she and the baby are in danger."

He looked up at Aaliyah. "She was in good health. What happened, when I left?"

"I have no explanation for her condition. She'll need to regain her stamina before we go farther. I have to level with you—one of them may not live. It's in the Most High's hands now. All we can do is pray."

"Pray if you must, but do as you've trained. You mustn't let her die." He whispered something to his favorite, and withdrew from the room.

The subsequent night, after a heroic fight, Yasmine delivered a stillborn boy. His father baptized, and named him Changa (*Strong like iron*). She held on for another day, but died in her sleep.

Before she could request a conference, gunmen escorted Aaliyah from the property and ordered her to never return. Abba Yisrael would never know, she suspected someone in the camp of committing murder.

The night of the uprising started off like any other. Most families were in their units preparing for bed. Men crammed in Abba Yisrael's inner sanctum, vehemently debated, the pros and cons of counter attacks.

The perimeter alarm rang.

"Take a deep breath. The exodus hour has arrived! You have your orders!"

Each retreated to his domicile, and readied his brood. Abba Yisrael retrieved everything vital from the underground vault then darted to his homes. He bid farewell to Lexine and his only son then ran off to inspect the exterior defenses.

At Batya's, situated a distance from the others, JoJo was alone. His spouse's absence didn't surprise him, as he'd not seen her in weeks. As soon as *"takeover"* whispers began, she started hiding valuables, and formulating her and Jacob's *"bolt"* plan.

When the alarm went off, the lovers jetted to their rendezvous point in the woods.

With zero time to waste, he washed her face then packed toys and changes of clothing in a bag. She yakked a mile a minute while he zipped between rooms. He also added a few items she wouldn't understand for safe keeping.

JoJo watched Abba Yisrael move about thinking he looked funny. She'd missed her father. "I'm happy you came to say hi!"

There was a loud commotion outside, followed by the pitter patter of feet. A man shouting his name became louder as he passed the bedroom window. He then knelt by her side. "Nakupenda (*I love you*), my star."

"Love you too, Baba. Are we going on a trip?"

He cupped her chin and thought—*Yasmine, my love. I miss you so much. I'm sorry I couldn't protect you and Joanna the way I promised. Thank you for watching over and guiding us.*

"Yes, my dear, you are. Baba must stay, and close the windows. Mind your manners."

"Okay. What time will I see you?"

If God willed it, he'd reunite with his flock in a few days, and they'd rebuild the homestead. He added his sash to the bag, and handed it to her, while fighting back tears. "It's important you keep this with you." There was a subversive in his camp who wanted his place and would assassinate him to take it. His youngest, was his only hope. This was possibly his last day on Earth. "I don't know, sweetheart. But you have my word—no matter what, I'll find you. Lexine will look after you until then."

"Okay. Yay! Hadara and Faven are my friends."

"Excellent! Then this should be fun."

"Yes, baba. I can't wait."

"Yasmine told me you were special."

"Close your eyes and believe what I tell you with all your heart." He pulled a rusty bike bell from his pocket. "Keep them closed."

"Okay."

"When you see me, and hear this sound again, you'll awaken. Usisahau (*Don't forget*)." He hit the lever three times in a row and pressed his pinky finger in the middle of her forehead.

"Baba, I'm hungry."

He chuckled. "All right, darling." With one foot out the door, he grabbed a few apples and corn muffins from the cupboard, and tossed them in the bag.

Outside, father and daughter found the pathways deserted. It pleased him to see the evacuation proceed as planned.

Before joining loyalists buttressing the main hall, he placed JoJo in a van at the front of the convoy. Worsening the panic, billows of opaque smoke rose from the rooves of their quarters. Disciples watched in horror as fire turned the night sky blood red. Men waving AKs banged on the bumpers and doors. Amazed drivers pulled away. Those inclined said devotions for the comrades left behind to preserve their heritage.

1

MOTHERS MATURE

02 OCT 1980—
WASHINGTON, D.C.

"What did you say?" asked Merle of her daughter Rosaria.

"This is Angie's baby girl, Joanna."

"Well—where's Angelique?"

"According to this letter, she passed four years ago."

She sat up in her chair. "What else does that letter say? Where's she been?"

"Mother, what's important is our new arrival needs a home."

The family had neither seen nor heard from the runaway in years. Private detectives surmised, with the measures she took to cover her tracks, Angelique didn't want to be found. Merle spent years angry with her eldest. Until now, she'd been denied verification of her demise.

With her right pointer extended, she instructed, "Come here, child." JoJo dropped her bag, and timidly walked forward.

"Let me look at you." She grabbed the frail girl's jaw, and studied her profile. With her strong bones and upturned eyes, she had little doubt they were kin.

Rosario looked on, praying she didn't spoil the pivotal moment. "Isn't she precious? That small mole is quite fetching too. I see Angelique all over her. It's incredible."

"I'd bet money her daddy's pure nigger."

"Mon Cheri (*my love*) be nice," chided an older gentleman

entering the room.

"What...Nice? *Hmmmh...* I'm being honest."

"Hello, cutie pie. What's your name?" asked Franklin, while patting JoJo's head.

Still unsure about the people surrounding her, she coyly replied, "JoJo."

"JoJo – *ahhhh.* Well, we're honored to meet you."

"Ni....nice to meet you, too."

"Belle!" screamed Merle, startling everyone.

"Yes, Madame....I'm here," answered the mousy-looking servant who'd appeared.

"Come here, gal! Quickly! This is my granddaughter. She will live with us. Please prepare the Rose room. Be sure to open the windows and change those sheets, as I'm sure you've not done this in some time. I also need you to thoroughly bathe this child. I'm certain there's a thousand miles of filth on her hands and feet."

Uncertain about which directive was the priority, Belle hovered in silence.

"What are you waiting for? Tend to the room."

"Yes ma'am....going now." She then exited as quietly as she entered.

"Jésus (*Jesus*), that girl is daft!"

"Merly—why must you be such a pill?"

"Je n'ai rien fait!" (*I didn't do anything!*). She's paid to work... not stand there and look dumb."

"At times, your rationale defies logic."

"Hmmmf!"

Franklin grabbed JoJo's hand. "Come. Let's have some of the tea and treats, the cook left for us."

She selected two from the assortment, and took a bite of a flaky confection.

He popped one in his mouth. "Bredeles. Aren't they splendid? They're my favorite; especially the ones with almonds.

"So good."

"Sit with me." She joined him on the Chesterfield. Happy to see a slight smile after sensing unease, he scooted closer. "How old are you, mademoiselle JoJo?"

"Seven."

"Seven years old. Isn't that something! You're such a big girl. I'm your grandpapa. You know—you look a lot like your mommy when she was your age. How time flies."

She leaned towards him. "You knew Yasmine?"

"Yasmine?"

"My mommy." Her voice was almost a whisper.

"Apparently, that was Angelique's new name." Merle confirmed.

"*Yaz-meen*.....*A-ha* that sounds exotic and mysterious. Is that Arabic?"

"Heaven only knows. Its tres' (*very*) uncouth if you ask me. Sounds like a name for one's aller aux putes (*whore*)."

He squinted, then shot Rosaria an exasperated glance. "No one asked you anything, Merle. Are you in need of a cocktail? How or why she became Yasmine is of no consequence. Our grandbaby is here now—look at her. She's a doll. And no matter what …she's family, and Pierre's care for our own."

2

GREET EXPECTATIONS

NINE YEARS LATER

*I*t was the height of election season and the dining room was full of lobbyists vying for the incumbent's time. The help had been moving since five a.m., setting up workstations and replenishing refreshments.

This was the most contentious race Franklin ever faced. A newcomer's message of *"draining the swamp"* and *"term limits"*, electrified swatches of his reliably conservative district.

The prospect of losing his influence and stature became real, when non-partisan polls showed a challenger, within the margin. Far too acquainted with winning, he initially scoffed at the neophyte's zeal.

"My constituents believe a bird in the hand is better than two in a bush and know what they're getting with F. James Pierre."

Merle, on the other hand, unearthed information, called in favors, and schemed to recapture the lead. All was going as planned, until the eleven o'clock news aired.

By nine a.m., she'd been on the phone, with his executive assistant, for an hour. The repetitive pen-tapping indicated her readiness to snap. Few knew with whom they were dealing. Her typically unruffled demeanor made her wrath even scarier.

JoJo had eavesdropped throughout the night. From the clamor, she gathered, the Senator caused a *"wreck in Eagle Harbor."* More than once, *"Scotch"* and *"twenty-five year old whore"* came out of her mouth as roars.

"The press are calling and I wanna make sure we present a unified front." After a pause… "Truth Shmuth! Your job is to keep people focused on the next legislative debate, an upcoming ribbon cutting ceremony or graduation, and his decades of successful Veterans initiatives. *Capeesh!* Must I also tell you how to communicate this? At this moment, your past achievements are irrelevant. Clean this up! My husband has his flaws, but I'll be the only one to leak or exploit them."

She tiptoed up the servant staircase to her bedroom. While she knew the details were juicy, this wasn't the first time her grandfather was up shit's creek. He routinely found himself embroiled in controversy, and experience had taught her, one thing for certain, and two things for sure—

1: Franklin wasn't going anyplace,
2: Merle will make the problem disappear, and
3: Life would go on, as usual.

Grandpop was one of her favorite people. Kind and patient— he was the ying (*peace*) to Merle's yang (*war*). When she was young, they solved puzzles, watched old Westerns, and put on puppet shows. His approachability made the early days bearable. He listened, encouraged, and never judged her, no matter what she disclosed.

Now that she was older, they had less in common.

She knew nil about marriage, but recognized Merle treated her spouse like a gofer. To the grassroots, his word was law. At home, he was consistently overridden. On more than one occasion he cried, *"You don't respect me!"*

Sadly, JoJo agreed. *How can anyone look up to a man so easily brought to his knees?*

Merle cranked him up, and pointed him in the direction she needed him to march. With her controlling the purse, his movements were restricted, and so were his thoughts.

Drills and activities once cluttered her calendar as well, but nowadays, JoJo had it relatively easy. As long as she didn't cause embarrassment, Merle left her alone. JoJo wasn't interested in tradition or the family business. Outside of church on Sunday, the *old bat*'s interest in her was minimal.

Eager to please, she used to jump at the click of her grandmother's heels. Now, she felt—

What's the point when she hates me?

I can't wait until I turn eighteen.

I'm going to run so far away from here, no one will find me.

They won't care. I've been a problem, since I appeared.

In the eighth grade, a school counselor, referred them to a doctor who diagnosed JoJo with Attention Deficit Disorder. *"Her daydreaming, constant need to move, and flight of ideas can be remedied with Ritalin."* The medicine caused tics and made her sleepy, so she lied when asked about taking them. Instead, she sold her monthly supply to finance her daily excursions.

Dismissal from a private, then a public school, pushed Merle over the edge. To prevent the *"situation"* from ballooning, she hired an expert to tutor JoJo at home. Dr. Juanita McDowell, whipped the undisciplined, but gifted girl into shape. Two years later, she had her diploma and was taking AP courses through the community college. The transformation pleased Merle. It enabled her to toot her own horn.

On days like this, JoJo thought it was best to stay out of the way. And considering the size of *Barf Manor*, the task was relatively simple. After years of losing herself in the maze of wings and rooms, she'd examined every cranny and nook. The window treatments, chandeliers, furnishings, art, and marble floors, were striking, but always felt icy, and uninviting.

Away from her grandmother's prying eyes, an attic storage room became her favorite place to hide. Early on, she suspected someone else had prized the rafter's privacy.

She forgot to duck as she climbed under her preferred dormer. The crack sent her to the floor. When she tried to rise, her palm dislodged a loose plank. Under it was a collection of R&B

cassette tapes, several Jet magazines, a small manila envelope of marijuana, rolling papers, pictures, and a leather-bound journal. A cardstock strip inscribed with "A.M.P." jutted out of the top. She knew the initials stood for Angelique Marie Pierre.

JoJo took the book from the niche. A photo fell onto her lap. It was *Yasmine*, around her same age. She kissed it, and with a mixture of sorrow and anticipation, read the opening passage:

October 26, 1972

My name is Angelique Marie Pierre, and today I turned sweet sixteen! I had an awesome day! You were a gift that came in the mail from Gramma Essie with a note. "For your dreams, EB." Janie snuck you in, and put you under my pillow. Mother would never approve or she'd demand to read it. I could hardly wait until I was alone so I could begin telling you about myself. I'm happy to have someone I can confide. I promise to tell you everything. As I write on your pages, I feel like I'm talking to a friend. For that reason, I shall name you Charlene.

Words couldn't adequately describe how much discovering her mother's sentiments raised her spirits.

"October 26, 1973. My name is Angelique Marie Pierre, and today I turned sweet sixteen!"

"We're the same age."

She scrolled to the succeeding entry. Also written in perfected script.

October 29, 1972

Dear Charlene,

I read a book written by a professor from Howard, The Bluest Eye. I'm forever changed.

"Joanna!" Merle screamed.

I hate when she calls me that! She returned the diary, and promptly left the room. Although she was eager to continue reading, it was more vital her honeycomb hideout remain hidden.

"Joanna Pierre!"

3

GRIN & BEAR

"**Y**es, Mam. I'm here."

Merle stopped digging through her hope chest and cast her eyes towards the ceiling. "Where are you always running off too? If I didn't know any better I'd think you had a portal to Narnia. Is your number ready for the lodge's anniversary? I'd like to see it."

"Now?"

"Yes, now! Why else would I have called you? I'll be in the parlor waiting for you. Don't dally. I have little time to spare."

JoJo turned to go to her room.

Almost every time I'm in this woman's company, she says something rude. Please—not today!

She'd already tried to weasel her way out of this year's show, but Merle made it clear, participation wasn't optional. Independent study didn't excuse JoJo from civic-related duties. Phone banking, get out the vote, and coat drives were fine but variety acts and prancing in pumps were torture. She resented having to play a role.

Fifteen minutes later, JoJo returned in a white leotard with a sequin belt around her waist, carrying a boom box. She usually played the recorder, but this year, dared to be different.

Merle sat in a wingchair near the window with her arms crossed, looking more than a little perturbed. She didn't care for surprises.

JoJo stretched, pressed "PLAY," and *"I Will Always Love You"* filled the room. The choreography for the interpretive dance, took a month to develop and learn. She and Belle, spent weeks practicing the intricate moves of the bridge and dramatic finale. Her arm and head movements, were nimble, and she knew her footwork was clean.

Despite her shyness around Merle, Belle, whom JoJo idolized, was no church mouse. Being a third generation "domestic," she knew better than to talk back. Part of the job was knowing when to shut up. The employer's word is law. Outside of work, she was a talented performer. That's where her personality mattered. She deserved a lot of credit for humbling herself in an unnecessarily tense environment.

When the song, ended Merle stared in silence before saying, "Interesting." Used to her noncommittal responses, JoJo wasn't offended.

"Who's singing? I recognize the melody."

"It's from the movie, The Body Guard. Whitney Houston is the singer and the leading actress. And, by the way, Dolly Parton loves this rendition."

"Whoever it is turned a simple, heartfelt, Country ballad into something...dare I say, Black. I detest jungle music."

"Don't you remember the commercial? Your favorite, Kevin Costner, is in it?"

"Oh yes! That's one striking man. I recall the gal now. Her mother is the gospel singer, Sissy Houston. Now—that's a great voice." She sipped her tea, and looked JoJo over. "A little less gyrating and swinging your arms would be nice, but all in all, not bad. With more practice and a new outfit, I suspect you won't embarrass me completely."

"Well, we wouldn't want that. Is there anything else?" JoJo collected her things.

"No—you may go. Oh! One more thing. Ask Robert to bring the car around. I need to go to Pentagon City."

"Yes, grandmother. I'll tell him, right away."

The lukewarm reception and dismissal told JoJo all she needed to know—*I got dressed up and sweaty for this old hag to insult me!*

At times like this, she loathed Merle.

I can't wait for the Fête, and election season to end. Then, she can go back to her normal obsessions.

"Call Joyce and schedule an appointment for Friday morning. Proper ladies wear their hair pressed. Yours shall be trimmed and curled for the party. End of discussion. I'll tolerate no argument. With the dress and kitten heels I selected, you'll make a decent showing."

"Fine." She departed.

After a shower, JoJo retrieved her earlier find. The *reefer* and other treasures were left for another time. She settled into her bed, and ran a finger along the decorative embellishments. Doodles obscured the inside cover. She found two particularly special—a puppy with wispy fur and a pink collar, and a *china man* with a pointy hat. With slanted slits for eyes, a pajama suit and fish head slippers, the whimsical figure made her laugh out loud.

Drawn to look like both were in motion, the artist's skill was evident, despite the simplicity of the renderings. She could picture Yasmine painting. She smelled and rubbed the pages against her heart, imagining her mother's vibrations. Because she had so few, the recollection, was a blessing.

"private: DO NOT ENTER" in bold black ink, marked the first page. She didn't plan to stop reading, but the commandment gave her pause.

This may be my only chance to know more.

She re-read a few entries, before succumbing to sandman's grip.

She yawned. "Borrow The Bluest Eye A.S.A.P."

With the lights off, she committed the referenced book to memory.

The Bluest Eye
The Bluest Eye
The Bluest Eye

4

SANDLEWOOD & VANILLA

JoJo heard, *"Bonne chance! (Good luck!)"*, before Merle shoved her to the front of the bright stage. She'd reached the blue tape-marked "X" in the center when the lights dimmed to a soft glow. Applause erupted as the curtains creaked open. They calmed as the intro began.

Executed without flaws, the four and a half minute piece, impressed the frigid audience. Her final pirouette concluded with a clean, silent landing. At the end, she curtsied with the grace of a royal.

When she stepped off the dais, Merle looked pleased until the judge's marks were announced. *"First prize—Hailey James!"*

The granddaughter of Merle's rival used the same song.

That isn't my fault!

Although she'd trained to win, JoJo congratulated the victor. The performance honored her father, a casualty of Desert Storm. There wasn't a dry eye in the house when she shared the tune's import.

On the way home, Merle fussed about "stiffness" and how *"the number lacked flair."* JoJo found the criticism confusing and unfair. *As usual—I'm never a priority…she never expresses concern… just ridicule and dissatisfaction.*

I'm tired of feeling like a failure. Nothing's ever good enough.

It's always my fault.

It's not like I could've won anyway.

Belle will been proud.

The diary couldn't have come at a better time.

With each passing year, her mother's smile became more of a blur. Merle never shared stories, polished her nails, told her she was pretty, or voiced love. Empathy and affection were all she wanted. JoJo could have been her biggest admirer, but her orneriness, made that impossible.

January 16, 1973

Dear Charlene,

My life in one word—Predictable. It's a never ending cycle of routine and rituals. There's something going on every day & night of the week. More and more, I find myself wanting to lounge on the couch and watch TV. This drives mommy crazy. My friends are the kids of judges, politicians, attorneys, and merchants. We attend private schools, have drivers and attend the same parties at the homes of other RBKs. We're members of the same social clubs and get grounded for the same stuff—breaking curfew, kissing boys, piercing our ears and tattoos (Minnie Jones). We had our cotillions at the same time, double date, vacation in Carr's each August and will apply to the same colleges (legacy, Ivies and top HBCUs).

I HATE IT.

I WILL NEVER BE WHO THEY WANT ME TO BE.

JoJo thought aloud, "I can relate to that!"

January 16, 1973

Dear Charlene,

I'm glad to be home. 2 weeks is the longest I ever stayed. When mother took me to the asylum, I felt an emptiness in my stomach that spread up my throat to the back of my eyes. I begged her not to leave me there, but she didn't care. I panicked when she said goodbye. I didn't cry even though I probably would have felt better afterwards. I need to hold on to that pain so I won't make the same mistake again.

A.M.P

Back home? Asylum?

January 18, 1973

Everyone is home except for Janie. Mommy says she's on leave. I can't wait for her to come back so we can catch up. There's no one to talk to when she's off. Rosaria tells daddy everything we discuss. She gets on my last nerve. We aren't talking right now. It's her fault they sent me to St. Elizabeths in the first place. I'll never forgive her for running her mouth. I know I said I wanted to kill myself but it was just talk. Sure—I get sad, but I know things will change once I leave for college. She wouldn't understand. I'm just a 'complainer'. I almost feel sorry for her.

To make matters worse, my so called best friends aren't returning my phone calls. What else can go wrong?

A.M.P

February 08, 1973

Dear Charlene,

M.B.P. is the biggest snob on this planet. Can you believe she told me I can't take up photography? It looks so cool. Why doesn't she understand I have my own interests?

Thank God she hasn't run Janie off. She's my saving grace. While technically she's my nanny, she's also my best friend. I'm Angel, and Rosaria's, her Little Rosy. She raised us to know we are special. Speaks French fluently (which mama loves), makes a mean gumbo, and shares "some" of her books. I snuck and read a chapter of the romance novel she's currently reading, The Kadin, by Bertrice Small.

My face is still red.

A.M.P

February 13, 1973

My dearest friend Charlene,

I've been so miserable. I can't even bear to write. I'll simply say—they fired Janie.

Now, I'm alone.

A.M.P

April 28, 1973

Dear Charlene,

The Pierre household is one of arrogance and self-loathing. On one hand, our story is one of achievement. On the other, my pride in "Black" identity is disrespectful. Mommy is so preoccupied with public perception and abhors the Black Power Movement. She hates that I'm into it. The 70's are an exciting time to be young. The racial conflict of the prior generation has passed. We enjoy levels of equality never thought possible. Optimism and hope are at an all-time high. What's wrong with my family? If I hear "second class citizen" one more time – I'll scream.

How did I end up with these parents?

I'm so frustrated. Time for a doobie.

A.M.P

May 08, 1973

Dear Charlene,

I've spent a lot of time around influential Black people and have come to believe wealth and ignorance are linked. Willful indifference is what one scholar called it. I hadn't reflected on it, until a homework assignment forced me to accept reality. I've been ignorant of struggle. I seek out those different from me. They make me feel alive.

Attending an HBCU in the Deep South has always been a dream, but Merle torpedoed the decision. "That's unacceptable!" is her only reason. I yearn to meet brothers and sisters from all over the globe—kids from rough and rural communities, military brats and those raised in single-parent homes.

Is it weird to hunger for bonds with those who grew up less fortunate than me?

I wish to create my own destiny. New energy is needed.

A.M.P

December 12, 1973

Dear Charlene,

Where do I start?

It's been months since I've written, but I couldn't put my mental state into words. I thought my mind was playing tricks on me, but now I know it wasn't a dream. For some reason, I feel guilty-like it's my fault. I have no one to talk to....no one can make it stop. He gets drunk, and babbles about how he's not the war hero he claims to be. A man who actually died in the battle of Adwa hunts him. I do not understand what any of this means. In the morning, we go on as usual.

A.M.P

JoJo gasped before moving to the next passage.
What the hell?
Who?

February 14, 1974

<u>Love Note to Self</u>:

You're young, Black, gifted and free. Be the change you want to see. You're strong, brave, and wise. Defy the odds and uplift humanity. You're the maker of your destiny, for you are a Goddess personified—dynamic black queen.

June 3, 1974

Dear Charlene,

I walked over the bridge to Anacostia today (mommy would faint) and saw the most exquisite man. Tall, dark and dashing. He spoke words that penetrated my heart. When he looked my way, I melted. I pray he'll take me away.

A.M.P

On the bottom of the page was a symbol, outlined so heavily it embossed the paper. Under it was the word "*hatima*" in capital letters.

March 14, 1974

Dear Charlene,

He was in my room last night. I'm not a little girl imagining things. This was real. Before I knew it, he'd inserted his hand in my panties and began rubbing it hard against my skin. I was numb. I stayed there because I forgot how to move. After he ejaculated, he wiped his hands on a towel draped on my desk chair and left. I cried and asked God, why me? I told mommy. In retrospect, I realize how incoherent my words must have been. Her face said she understood, but didn't care.

I'll kill them, if I don't leave here soon.

I know where the guns are kept.

A.M.P

March 23, 1974

"Birds born in a cage think flying is an illness."
—Alejandro Jodorowsky

March 26, 1974

If I had a daughter, I'd tell her to let nothing or anyone hold her back. To exude confidence even when afraid. And to know her greatest threat is herself. She'll know I wanted and loved her more than air. Why birth a child to hurt them? That's a phenomenon I'll never understand.

For me? Wow!

April 1, 1974

Dear Charlene,

I suppose I was around 5 when it started happening. He called it "tickling." I touched him. He told me, 'you don't know how good that makes me feel.' Yuck!

I thought I was ready to write more.

I hate him.

A.M.P

May 13, 1974

Dear Charlene,

I heard mommy and daddy fussing about me last night. Since I told her about what he did, she stares at him with disgust. It didn't stop him from "visiting" me a few hours later. Only bright spot in my life—he's gone for a month.

A.M.P

JoJo read *The Bluest Eye* in two days. The heartbreaking story was hard to follow, but made sense upon reflection. Much like the protagonist, JoJo prayed for love, and wondered if Merle would be nicer if she were prettier, or lighter. Unlike Pocola, she didn't fear hunger, or closing her eyes at night, yet she was just as dispirited, knowing she'd never meet the Pierre's standards, or feel secure.

The girl sulking in family portraits was still an enigma. Despite knowing her intimate thoughts, the only thing she better understood was her gloom.

She drifted off, wondering if her dad was the man mentioned.

"I walked over the bridge to Anacostia today (mommy would faint) and saw the most exquisite man. Tall, dark and dashing. He spoke words that penetrated my heart. When he looked my way, I melted. I pray he'll take me away."

Dark...

JoJo never forgot Merle's comment. *"I'd bet money her daddy is pure nigger."* Since then, she learned the word meant poor, black, and ignorant.

Baba, she recalled, was a burly man with a bald head. His facial features were fuzzy, but she'd never forget his dimples.

It surprised her to think of them, after so many years.

Yasmine's spirit visited her while she slept. At first, she didn't recognize her, but her signature fragrance, Sandalwood and Vanilla, was unforgettable. She reached out, and softly stroked JoJo's thigh. Her caress felt sublime. As she parted her lips to speak, a movement roused her. She opened her eyes, but quickly closed them. Franklin stood at the foot of her bed in long johns, cradling a bottle of Dewar's. With glassy eyes, he mumbled something indistinguishable to the monster haunting him. He left a half hour later without touching her.

Afterwards, she sat up processing the knowledge that Franklin was a molester. It was his house, but being in her room in the middle of the night wasn't right. She was also angry about not getting to hear what her mother wanted to say.

5

GONE GIRL

T he next morning when Belle arrived, Merle fired her without explanation. Sadly, her prediction rang true. *"I won't be around here forever."* JoJo wished she'd understood what she meant at the time, and told her how much she loved her.

Hours later, anger replaced the sorrow, as she rehashed her and Merle's subsequent spat. It quickly went from bad to worse. Neither party held back.

"Get over it! Her services are no longer needed. You're old enough to fend for yourself. I think it's time you took on more responsibility... And if you step out my door without permission—don't come back. I'm not dealing with your insolence."

She told Merle about Franklin being in her room.

If she cared, she didn't show it.

"We gave you a place to stay. You could be living on the streets. Your ways will land you in jail one day, and those bull daggers will eat you alive. No pun intended!"

"Jail? Bull daggers? What are you talking about? This house? It means nothing to me. I don't need any of this?"

"You're such an ingrate—immoral and utterly worthless like your mother. Maybe, you're bi-polar too? Perhaps we should've left you with those spear chucking gypsies. You'd probably fit right in."

"You're both miserable souls who deserve one another. Your husband is a devil and you're his ice queen."

"You'll not cause me heart burn. If you don't cease your whining

27

and disrespect, you can follow her example and leave."

JoJo tucked towels under her door and turned on the ceiling fan. After opening the window, she propped large pillows against the wall, sat down, lit a joint and dived into the diary from the beginning. This time, she endeavored to read between the lines. *What are you saying?*

Pencil drawings, the names of foreign destinations, and elaborate gowns, covered sixty percent of the tome. Victorian-age bodices, petticoats, and flowing trains floated off the pages. Most inscriptions were short and lighthearted, but some were intense and descriptive. Her estrangement from family and desire for adventure, mirrored JoJo's discontentment.

With each pass of the sepia-tinted sheets, resentment for her guardians increased. The love and hatred she held for her discovery were equal. A quest for answers opened a Pandora's Box of abuse, betrayal, and deceit.

Though there were few entries, *Angelique* painted a bleak picture. Tears poured from JoJo's eyes, as she realized she had no idea what to do with this information. Once the initial shock passed, she felt compelled to do something drastic. The last log read like a call-to-action:

June 5, 1974

Dear Charlene,

After considering my options….living in this house is no longer possible. No girl should have to satisfy her father. Money is the least of my concerns. I refuse to lose my mind. I'm going to follow my heart.

Angelique

JoJo got up, leaned over her desk, and scribbled on a piece of paper, "I'm no liar or charity case." She filled a small suitcase on wheels with underwear, toiletries, and clothes. The dresses and other *frilly shit* Merle liked were left alone.

She smiled, glad everything fit in one bag.

Hatima, she learned, meant destiny.

Eighteen is too far! They never wanted me any way!

To hell with the Pierres.

I am worthy of more!

Deprived of her mother's firsthand account of life, she would've underestimated their level of depravity.

They drove my mama crazy…chased her away.

She couldn't imagine things getting any better.

With five hundred and forty dollars, a book of McDonald's gift certificates, a few photos and *Angelique's* memoir in the knapsack strapped to her back, she whispered "ciao" to her room.

If need be—I'll walk all night, and sleep during the day.

I'll figure something out.

I just need to go – Today!

Clasping the suitcase to her chest, she crept down the back stairs, then passed through a small hallway. Her grandparents sat in the parlor. Crumpling newspaper and soft giggles were the only signs of either's presence.

Greta was busy prepping dinner, and didn't notice her slip out the back door. She normally slept late on Thursdays. Her absence could go unnoticed until the afternoon.

As JoJo approached a mailbox, she considered addressing an envelope to the police.

'Come sit on grandpop's lap!'

Eww!

'Hide those bee stings when you go out.'

He's sick! Has he been grooming me the whole time?

She opened and closed the shoot, a few times, before reneging. Finding a tangible connection to her mother was luck. Prosecuting Franklin wasn't satisfying enough to give the magic up.

JoJo strolled through DuPont Circle, peering into the large

windows. She'd been there numerous times and knew the shops with the best stuff. *Booktropolis* was also a few steps away from the large Baroque fountain on Massachusetts Avenue. She thought of stopping in before hitting the library. She'd seen people napping in their quiet rooms, and planned to assess the feasibility of her doing the same.

She'd started her trek to the quirky bookstore when a blond fellow dressed in tan khaki slacks, navy and white checkered shirt, and burgundy bow tie, disrupted her stride. "Excuse me, miss. May I help you?"

She ignored him and kept walking.

He called louder. "Wait! Not so fast! Stop!"

"No thanks. I'm okay." She picked up her pace.

A patrolman at a nearby hot dog cart, heard the commotion and saw her reaction. He stepped onto the median strip. "Is there a problem?" She was half way down the block when he yelled, "Hold up! Freeze!"

She contemplated running, but felt her chances were better if she kept cool, and appealed to reason. *I've done nothing wrong.*

The shopkeeper and officer, moved towards her.

"What's going on?" asked the officer, of no one specifically.

Before JoJo could utter a word....

"As you know, there has been a rash of crash and dash robberies in the area. She looks like the girl, we've identified as a shoplifter."

"What? I didn't do anything. You asked 'may I help you' and my answer was no. Where do you get off implying such a thing? You didn't see me doing anything other than minding my business! I'm no damn thief. If I'm a thief, you're a bigot." She then turned to the officer. "Is it against the law to look in windows?"

Instead of answering, he asked, "Do you have identification?"

"What? But I'm the one getting harassed."

"Good day, officer." The smug man affirmed, before retreating to his haberdashery. JoJo blurted, without thinking, "Go to hell...

you Bart Simpson lookin'..."

"Eh!" barked the officer. "You better calm down and produce some ID, pronto!"

An older Caucasian woman exited her boutique, carrying a piece of paper. She addressed him by name. "Officer Yates. It's not the girl. Take a look at the photo on the most recent blotter. It's not even close. I saw everything. Martin's a bit overzealous. The gal's telling the truth. She only looked in the window. Let the young lady go on."

The policeman observed her with skepticism before responding. "Thanks, Patty." He'd started to address JoJo when something over the radio, caused him to pause, and turn red. The frantic officer screamed, while darting to his car. "Get gone! I don't wanna see you around here again!"

JoJo turned to the woman, and shook her head. "Thank you. I really didn't do anything wrong."

"I know you didn't. These are peculiar times we're living in."

"You can say that again."

"Would you like me to level with you?"

"Yes, of course."

"This probably isn't the best place to be an African-American girl, without supervision. Most of these shops are run by snobs unprepared for change. I hate to say it, but for you, the police are gonna be useless."

She didn't know what any of it meant, but her haughty tone reminded her of Merle. At the end of the day it didn't matter, she was free.

"You should get going."

"Thanks again."

"Have a good day, sweetie."

6

STEPPING STONES

PRINCE GEORGE'S COUNTY, MD

*I*t was day four of Nancy Mallory's first week on the job and this was her inaugural case. Having been a foster child herself, black girls were of special interest. She'd left corporate Finance two years before and got a Master's degree in Social Work for this very purpose. The former spokesmodel glided into the busy precinct, and confidently up to the front desk.

JoJo had been in the same spot for an hour.

Something's gotta give!

She noticed the svelte, bespectacled, stunner with skin the color of coal, the minute she walked into the room. Unlike the other officers she'd encountered, this one smiled and had style.

The conversation had the fat captain *cheesin' like a pizza.* Until now, he'd been grumpy and unhelpful. When the arrival unexpectedly pivoted in her direction, she bowed her head.

Oh, my god. Is she coming over here?

When she looked up again, the mystery lady looked down.

Nancy extended a manicured hand in greeting. "Hi Joanna. I'm CPS Agent Mallory or Miss Mallory, whichever you prefer. It's nice to meet you."

JoJo lifted her chin, but didn't speak.

Catching the drift, she pulled it back, and altered her approach. "Do you mind if I sit?"

"Not at all."

"My feet are killing me, but these shoes are too beautiful to not share. How are you holding up? I imagine you've had a long day."

"Yes—I have."

The run-in with Officer Yates rattled her, but fear wouldn't alter her plan. She stepped into the library, a few blocks away, and stayed until guards locked the doors at six for a private event.

With no place to go, she needed to sit, and regroup. The long benches along the National Mall popped into her head. She took Massachusetts Ave to 9th and paused at Mt. Vernon Square to catch her breath.

After sunset, the city she'd always loved, looked unfamiliar. The erratic lights, speeding cars, and blaring horns, overloaded her senses.

Many of the people she passed were creepy, and unfriendly. A crazy woman, occupying a bus stop, growled when she said, "Hi."

At Pennsylvania Avenue, a hobo nearly mowed her down. He hurried past, arguing with the air. Then, out of nowhere, he stopped his cart and peered over his shoulder. *Go home, stupid little girl! Nothing's good down there!"*

Down where? She wondered, but laughed it off.

A few minutes later, it started raining. With the Capitol dome in view, she took shelter under a steel structure, and swapped her docksiders for the rubber boots, she'd reluctantly added to her suitcase. Soon, a puddle formed at her feet. Wet, shivering, and caught up in her feelings, she didn't notice the policewoman's approach.

For whatever reason, she wouldn't buy the yarn about *"taking a breather."* It wasn't long before JoJo found herself in the back of a cruiser.

If she were being honest, she'd admit to being relieved. She expected it to happen, albeit not so soon.

Nancy snapped her fingers to recapture her new client's attention. "Tell me about yourself."

"An officer brought me snacks from the machine around eight o'clock but I haven't eaten since. And I prefer JoJo."

Nancy spoke slowly, determined not to react to the teen's moxie. *"Mmmm, k*—your name preference is noted. I'm not sure what I can do about food, this second, but I'll see what I can make happen. I need to chat with the officer in charge. I'll be back. "

As JoJo watched her prance to the front desk, she regretted her rudeness. In truth, Nancy had been the first to ask about her well-being.

Several hours passed before her grandmother picked up the phone. When she did, she calmly told them *"Joanna's on her own!"* Although she acted unfazed, Merle leaving her hanging stung.

JoJo ate a burger and fry combo, while Nancy drove in silence. She wanted to ask a million questions, but slouched in her seat and sipped her soda instead.

As they journeyed to their destination, the backdrop worsened. *Where are we headed?*

They stopped in front of a big house on a dark tree lined street. A wooden sign hung from a post—*Stepping Stones Transition Center.* The interior was dark except for a light in the front room. Before exiting the car, Miss Mallory prepped her for the next step. "This is where you'll stay until we can find something permanent." Noticing JoJo hadn't moved, she smiled. "There's no reason to worry. This is one of the nicer facilities in the area. It's operated by an older sista. We're lucky they had space for you."

"Okay." JoJo bit her fingernails, struggling to maintain control. As they moved closer, she felt a need to hurl.

Nancy cracked the screen door and knocked. "You'll be fine."

A clean shaven, short-haired black man who introduced himself as "*Mr. Franks*" received them. As they pass through the hall, he stopped at an open archway. She glanced inside and spied three couches with seventies-style green floral print, Formica top tables, lamps and shelves full of board games and magazines. Three teens sprawled across the chairs, rapt by an action sequence.

"This is our day room…. How's it going, guys?"

None of them reacted to his voice. He turned to her. "That's Jay, Marquis, and Kaori."

"Listen up! This is JoJo. I expect you to show her the ropes. And don't forget—shut 'er down at midnight! You've got about 30 more minutes."

The boys ignored him, but the girl looked up, and waved.

The trio continued until they reached an office where he pointed to a pew. "Have a seat."

The adults stepped inside. Five minutes later, Nancy emerged, looking drained. "Don't get up. I'm going, but I'll be back in a few days. Mrs. Grant, Mr. Franks, and Maurice will take care of you. Try to get some rest."

Although they'd only been together for a short time, JoJo wished she could stay. She'd been pleasant and made her feel safe. "Okay. I appreciate your help. When will I see you?"

"Can't say when, but soon."

"Okay. I appreciate all you've done."

Moments later, a stylish older woman entered, carrying a packet of papers, and humming a Chaka Khan tune. She unzipped her coat, smiled and handed JoJo the documents. "You must be Joanna. I'm Mrs. G. Welcome. Here's a schedule and our rule book. We'll go over them tomorrow. For now—follow me."

Fay Grant navigated the halls with awareness of the loose floorboards, shadowy bends and jutting furniture. JoJo trailed closely behind, amazed by how fast she moved. The petite powerhouse had always been underestimated because of her size. While a tough cookie, she rarely screamed or revealed her mean side. She and her deceased husband opened *Stepping Stones* fifteen years prior. Since his passing, she relied on two men she'd groomed to oversee the youth.

When they reached the top of the stairs, she stopped. "I like it quiet this time of the evening. There are seven in-residence. Our max capacity is ten."

They inched through a hallway, bypassing three doors, before stopping. Mrs. G led her into a dark room and turned on a bedside lamp. To her great surprise, twin desks, dressers and beds fit inside.

"*Shhhh*—that's Ramona buried under the covers. Shy girl. You'll meet her in the morning. There's a bathroom across the hall. Wiggle the handle when you flush. Breakfast is at eight. Follow the noise. Sleep tight, sweetie."

When she left, JoJo looked over at the stranger snoring like a freight train and thought, *it's gonna be a long night.*

7

TRAINING DAY

ONE WEEK LATER

*J*oJo wandered into the TV room, and a cluster of girls burst into laughter. She wondered why, until she saw Tina *stinking up* her zip-front hoodie.

Why me? She cast her eyes to the floor. *What kind of games is she playing?*

The grin on Tina's face dared her to buck. Her taut lips dripped with unearned satisfaction.

Ole pie-face finds this funny.

Kenesha and T'yese, a pair she already disliked, stood by her side. They engineered drama, and took indifference to their shenanigans, personally.

JoJo assumed a boxing stance. Tina threw her head back, and laughed. Her conspirators copied.

"That's my jacket."

"Nah—not anymore."

"Yes, it is." It was one of the few items she'd brought from home. And as much as she wore it, everyone knew it was her favorite.

Tina shortened the gap between them. "Well, if it is. I'm wearing it. Whatchu gonna do bout it?"

House rules required she report the breach, but wiping the smirk from Tina's face felt more urgent. After sizing up her opponent—*short, pudgy, enough naps to grip*—she concluded, *I can take her.*

She'd never felt cornered, and prepared to pounce, at the same time.

"I'm going to ask for it back–nicely. If that doesn't work, things may turn tragic. Either way, I'm ready. May I please, have my jacket?"

"You're gonna have to come get it, Mz. Badass. Don't make me…"

Midway through Tina's threat, JoJo socked her in the chin. Doubled over in pain and coughing, JoJo knocked her down, and straddled her. Five or six good licks later, she proceeded to ring her neck.

Watching them tango, was an education for her accomplices. They'd tried to lure JoJo into a confrontation, but she never paid them any attention.

Focused on not letting Tina flip her over, JoJo left an opening for T'yese to grab her hair. Kenesha attempted to free Tina, but JoJo's grip was too tight.

Other residents ran into the room and chanted—"Fight! Fight! Fight!"

T'yese and Kanesha's kicks and jabs stunned, but JoJo was in a zone. She kept drumming Tina until someone screamed, "Maurice and Mister Marcus are coming!"

Everyone broke their hold. Tina got up from the floor.

Before JoJo could make her next move, Tina swung, and caught her left temple. Droplets trickled from the gash. Blood smeared finger tips. Through blurred vision and a sudden burst of energy, she dived into her attackers, knocking both onto the couch.

Staffers moved in quickly to separate them. JoJo screamed as they dragged her to Mr. Franks' office. "Stop! Let me at them bitches! Get off of me!"

Combat wasn't something she sought, but knowing she could throw bows, if she had to, gave her strength. She knew she could go from zero to sixty, but had never blacked out. The way she heaved, shrieked and hit, were animalistic.

JoJo flexed her stinging knuckles.

Fighting hurts but I bet they won't underestimate me again.

Shame on them for awakening a beast!

From this point forward, she'd be the one telling people what to do. Her opponents had been bigger, but she was smarter, and more nimble. She'd never be the debutante her grandmother wanted her to be.

She'd be better.

I'm no victim, and I won't stand for bullying around me.

Despite the trouble she faced, she wouldn't complain. The wisdom gained, made up for the pain.

Before she knew it, weeks turned into months and *Stepping Stones* became home. The dwelling wasn't large, but Mrs. Grant kept things orderly and made prudent use of the space. They ate well, there was plenty to read, and a clinically depressed roommate, had its perks. Ramona talked little, didn't make a mess, and spent most days asleep.

Two days following their scuffle, T'yese packed her bags and departed. Kenesha was out a week later. Tina was still around, but JoJo laughed aloud whenever they crossed paths. *What a clown!*

Ms. Mallory's weekly updates kept her optimistic. The overworked agent, appreciated that JoJo wasn't a *"rebel rouser,"* like the bulk of her cases.

"Your situation is also—I'll say abnormal, for lack of a better word. Your grandmother will pay for our board, medical care, necessities, etc. That's a blessing. I have an idea I'm looking into. While I investigate, thank you for your patience. I've talked it over with Mrs. G, and you can live here as long as needed."

Little did either know—Mrs. Grant loved clients like JoJo. The Merle Barthe-Pierre's of the world never snooped, and preferred paying in advance.

These days, she was demerit free and adjusting to house procedures. She knew it was strange she didn't know how to scrub or use a mop, but she eventually got the hang of it.

At Merle's, she never did chores— *that's why I pay the maids.* Her least favorite chore was tending the cats. Two Persians lived at Barthe Manor, but she'd never cleaned up behind the *ghastly* beasts.

Monday's *"Game Night"* was followed by *"Taco Tuesday."* Wednesdays were "free" (some went to therapy), Thursdays were for movies, and Friday's highlight was *"Crafts with Mrs. G."*

On Saturdays, Maurice carried residents to the mall, or a public library, and Sundays were for worship. JoJo never went to church, but got a kick out of Jim and Tammy Faye Baker.

For those with jobs or in night school, curfew was at nine o'clock on weeknights and eleven on weekends and holidays. Around this time, *"mentors"* did their rounds then went ghost until morning.

On most evenings, if KD wasn't around, JoJo ate dinner, then watched TV until going to bed. Her road dog was Jeremy Herman, an awkward white teen with bad acne and dark, stringy hair. She called him the *'remote control commander'* because it was frequently in his hand.

Both of them loved *Wheel of Fortune*, *Dukes of Hazzard* and *Mama's Family.* He laughed when something was amusing, but for the most part, interacted as much as a clock. Neither brought up their personal lives. Company was all the other needed.

It was Thursday night—*"Must See TV."*

As the lineup got underway, JoJo felt a chill. To her dismay, the blankets were packed away for the season. During a commercial, she left to grab one from the basement storage. She opened the door, and eased down the narrow staircase. As she approached the tubs, masculine and feminine whimpers flooded her ears.

"Oh Shit, Ethan. *Mmmmh…*yes, daddy. I love it.…*mmmmh.* I'm coming."

"*Shhhhh!* Girl, lower your voice. I know this Johnson good

…this that grown man Mandingo cock…Yes, baby, yes! Damn. Let go!"

Then she heard a hand against bare flesh—"Pap…pap…. pap….pap!"

The boiler room door was slightly ajar. Compelled to take a peek, JoJo inched closer. Tina and Mr. Franks a/k/a *Ethan* semi-naked, and conjoined bodies, glistened under the fluorescent lighting. He delivered a round of deep plunges into her rear, before quickly pulling it out. "Here. Here. Here!" Tina turned around, got on her knees, and greedily sucked the staffer's dripping member. The strained howl that followed, was a mixture of shock and wonder.

After wrestling his dick from her mouth, Ethan helped her stand. She brushed some dirt and pebbles off her legs. They both sighed. He grabbed a handful of ass with one hand, pulled her closer with the other then kissed all over her face.

JoJo wanted to watch, but tip-toed upstairs. While absorbing all she'd observed, JoJo mused whether it repulsed or turned her on.

She sat on the couch and leaned forward. *That was gross!*

"Where'd you go? The first part of the show is over."

"Damn. What did I miss?"

"A whole lot, and the second half is ready to start. Where's the blanket?"

She'd forgotten about it. "Damn! You know—I'm not even cold anymore."

8

FOX IN THE HEN HOUSE

olitude was non-existent in a house full of people. Taking a dump without interruption was pure luck or the result of strategic thinking. JoJo had been holding it all day and was ready to drop when she noticed something significant missing.

"Who uses all the toilet paper and leaves the empty roll? Shit!" cursed JoJo before pulling up her panties, then jeans. The last thing she wanted to do was talk to '*Ethan*'.

Mrs. G's personal life was in crisis. Her youngest, got shot in Southeast DC. Consequently, she took some *"personal time,"* and she spent visiting hours at the hospital. The *"good kid getting mixed up with the wrong crowd"* trope is always tragic. While his mother fostered others' children, her own suffered from instability. Equal part conceit and naiveté, led her to believe her sons were immune to the allure of the projects.

In her absence, Mr. Franks was in control, and thus he held the Charmin.

After several weeks, she still couldn't get his and Tina's image out of her head. *Him*, drooling and grunting, and *her*, throwing ass and braids back like a pro. She giggled whenever he passed, but felt stupid later. Nothing was humorous. The reaction was 100% nerves.

To the masses, he was a principled, upstanding citizen. A man the State entrusted with vulnerable children. But JoJo recognized a skillfully constructed front. His radiant smile masked the machinations of a predator.

No one else noticed Tina and Mr. Franks, routinely disappearing without reason. Their faces and body language bore the evidence of regular entanglement. Neither, were new to this taboo.

The rest of the staff were only there for a pay check. Mr. Marcus, Ms. Paula and Ms. Terry, spent more time entwined in their love triangle than caring for their charges. Maurice's family and Mrs. Grant attended the same church. The mama's boy did nothing but drive the van, scratch his balls, sniff his fingers and eat up the snacks. A couple of college students worked on weekends, but they were just as toothless.

Tina still cut her eyes whenever they entered the same room, but at least JoJo knew why—*she's feeling herself.*

Filling a hole in the heart, makes girls do silly things.

She kept her mouth closed about what she'd seen from the shadows and prayed for the angry, misguided teen. Validation of what she witnessed wasn't essential.

As long as he's fixated on Tina, he isn't thinking about me.

He didn't make sexual advances, but paid her extra attention. She wasn't dumb. Concern for her *"safety"* didn't warrant the added scrutiny.

The first level buzzed with an inordinate amount of activity. For the prior couple of months, teens came and left the group home daily. JoJo didn't interact with any of them.

She peeked into the day room. Two sneaky-looking boys caught her eye. The stoned gaze of one, and goofy smile plastered on the other's mug, were dead giveaways. *They're high as shit!* She knew the look well, and had been guilty of her own unwitting disclosures.

One evening as she sat on the couch, a book of rolling papers, slipped out of her pocket. Kaori (pronounced *Corey*) or KD, as she preferred, tapped her on the shoulder and smiled. Until this point they'd spoken little, so she didn't know how she'd carry it. To her shock, she pulled a dime of bud from her sock. The two snuck off to a nearby park, then smoked and laughed, until their stomachs hurt.

"*Me neva would've imagined Miss Proper puffed da ganja,*" joked KD as she passed the blunt.

"*Miss Proper? Please. I e-nun-ci-ate my words. That's all.*"

"*I know, but it's rare. For that alone, I like you.*"

From that day they were close. With a friend, JoJo felt a little safer.

Sneakers and *The Bullets* were shared interests. Both dreamed of viewing a buzzer beater from half-court. JoJo wished she had a third of her poise. Nothing frazzled, or made her raise her voice. Though only a few months older, her humility and demeanor, made her appear more mature.

At seventeen, she already had a federal job. "*Hand it over to the Lord!*" was her solution for every problem. Everything from her choice of words, manner of dress, and diverse hobbies, challenged convention. Well-versed in music, art and literature, JoJo found a kindred spirit.

Both saw group home living as "*abnormal,*" and knew it messed with some kids' heads. Rather than complain, they reminded each other, they were blessed, to not be chained to "*Uncle Lester's*" bed.

Talk of her existence pre-D.C. had been forbidden. Mother Goose rhymes and religious hymns replaced songs about freedom, unity and love for brown skin.

"*Brainwashing,*" "*voodoo,*" *and* "*campfire orgies,*" were engrained in her head. In spite of the forecasted doom, she *still* pondered what it meant.

If she mentioned Yasmine, Baba or the Nation, Merle went off—

"*I don't want to hear anything about that Back to Africa cult. Push that rubbish out of your mind!*"

KD listened. She'd never heard of Yahweh, Israel or any of the other words that arose from her latent memory, but admitted, it was fascinating.

They talked about getting a place together when both turned eighteen. JoJo couldn't wait to be free.

Outside the office, her heartbeat quickened in anticipation of the exchange. She knocked, and waited for Mr. Franks to answer. She heard people inside arguing in hushed voices. Tina stepped out, and she stepped in. As their arms brushed, Tina mumbled. "Bitch!"

"Mr. Franks. I need toilet tissue? The upstairs lavatory is out."

Without looking away from his computer monitor, he handed her a roll. "Please shut the door behind you."

She complied, glad he didn't say more.

Tina was standing at the end of the hall seething with her arms crossed. Sensing hostility, JoJo walked close to the wall.

"Must be nice to be on a first name basis with the admin. Have a great day."

She would regret making the snarky statement, but smacking the contempt off Tina's face, made the ultimate price, fair.

"Whatever!"

She stormed into the office, minus knocking, and slammed the door.

9

EMANCIPATION

While waiting for the van, JoJo read the headlines and horoscopes. When the horn sounded, she tossed the newspaper on the end table, and smoothed imaginary wrinkles out of her chinos.

Standing in the hallway mirror, her confidence was on ten. The narrow points of her shoes pinched, but looked too stylish to complain. Plus, Ms. Mallory was kind for buying them.

Following several overcast days, the morning dawned clear and sunny. Nature's voices formed a symphony of ambient noise. She leapt off the porch, into a warm breeze. The deep breath she inhaled before climbing inside, felt cleansing.

Mrs. G sat high in the passenger seat. She joyfully delivered her customary greeting, "Smile. This is the day Jehovah made. Let us rejoice, *hammercy*, and be glad in it!" Typically clad in a t-shirt and jeans, she dazzled in brown leggings and vest, tan blouse with a bow collar, riding boots, and turquoise jewelry.

Comforted by her presence, JoJo giggled.

"You look nice, Miss Pierre."

"You too, Mrs. G! Thank you. I'm happy to see you."

"I wouldn't let you face today alone." Maurice accelerated up the block. She shot him a disapproving glance. "Don't forget buckle your seat belt."

They trio reached the town center in thirty minutes. Gridlock slowed their pace from the off-ramp, as camera crews, watchdogs, and activists converged on the county. A trial of National interest, was underway in the Circuit Court building.

To avoid being late, JoJo and Mrs. G hopped out the van a block away.

As they crisscrossed the street, Ms. Mallory and a therapist, she'd seen twice, waved to gain their attention. With ten minutes to spare, both had questions to ask, and points they wanted to raise. JoJo's palms were sweaty. Anxiety crept into her chest. She didn't know all of what *"Emancipation"* entailed, but inferred it meant, legally she'd be an adult. When the speeches were finished, the group marched towards the entrance.

Merle Barthe-Pierre stood outside the Master's Chamber. She and JoJo nodded in the other's direction, electing not to speak or embrace.

The proceeding was straightforward with nothing contested on either side. When called to the stand, the judge asked about her grades in school, employment history, and others questions to assess her state of mind. When it came time for her to explain how she'd care for herself, Merle stepped forward and whispered something in Nancy's ear.

She then passed a piece of paper to the bailiff, who gave it to the judge. The letter provided details of a trust fund *"available for withdrawal at eighteen years, and nine months."*

JoJo was dazed.

"In addition to the first $150,000, she'll receive another $150,000 on her twenty-fifth and $200,000 on her thirtieth birthdays."

Following the tap of the justice's gavel, she skimmed through the stack of papers she'd been handed. A Social Security Card and Birth Certificate were among the collection.

This was the first time she'd ever considered its existence.

"Joanna Pierre; 22 November 1973; Mother: Angelique Pierre; Unmarried. Father: Unknown. Birthplace: Chester, Virginia."

The date and location of her birth, were always subjects of contention. The only thing she'd known for certain was she'd been born. There were few bombshells, which surprisingly hurt.

A lump formed in her throat.

Mrs. Grant approached, looking worried. "Are you, okay?"

"I'm fine." She lied, still unsure, why she felt frustrated. "This has been a long day. I'm ready when you are." She secured the flap on the envelope and pushed away from the table.

As they emerged from the building, Merle, sat on a bench, close to the door. She motioned for JoJo to join her. "Take all the time you need, sweetie. We'll be in the van."

"Thanks. I won't be long." Though she hadn't processed all she'd heard in court, she figured a parting word couldn't hurt.

"How've you been, Joanna?"

"I'm fine."

"That's nice to hear."

"What about you? How's the family?"

"All of us are well. Rosaria wanted to be here, but stayed home with a sick little one." Merle elected not to mention, Franklin sent his love. "Here's some money. Please buy yourself something to eat. They've assured me you're fed three meals daily, but you look gaunt."

JoJo assumed this was the last time she'd see her grandmother. Instead of countering her cruel comment, she vowed to say something positive. "I want you to know I appreciate you taking me in when I was a little girl. It was fun growing up in such a beautiful house."

Warmed by the compliment, she gently seized JoJo's chin. "That's nice of you. Joanna, for what it's worth, I hope you find the happiness you seek." Merle kissed her on the cheek and wished her granddaughter the best of luck. A black car stopped at the curb. "That's my cue."

The driver got out, and waited. Before leaving, the relatives shared an extended hug.

There's so much more I wish I'd said.

As the sedan blended into traffic, her grandfather waved from the rear window. She returned the gesture. She'd learned from the paper, his re-election bid had been spurned.

He was a shell of a man... liable, *at any second,* to fall apart. *Poor Franklin—Merle's probably giving him the blues.*

10

SCREAM

"You've got thirty days. I need your bed. If you're not gonna pay rent– you gots to leave!"

"But Mr. Franks, I have nowhere to go."

"That's not true. Maurice told me about the dough you're getting and the rich old lady you were talking to outside the courthouse."

"Going is the operative word." JoJo didn't plan on touching the Pierre's money, but that was none of his business.

They pray I'll use it to vanish.

Just give me a little time; no bribe or incentive required.

Her mother walked away from it, and she'd do the same.

Ethan pointed one of his long fingers at the open doorway. "Going, got or gone. Makes me, no never mind. If you're not paying, I need to find someone who will."

"Why are you being so cold?"

"It's a cold, cold world, young one…especially for those as stuck up as you. Best you learn now. Don't blame me for telling you the truth."

"What's that supposed to mean?"

He licked his lips. "I perused your file. You's a smart girl. Figure it out. I'm sure if you thought about it, you'd come up with something to make us both happy."

She felt zero attraction and playing along made no sense. *There has to be a way to make him back off that doesn't involve sex.* She left the room angry, but feeling defeated. The rickety aluminum screen door slammed, and she charged downed the front steps. At the bottom she put her hands on her hips, and tilted her head upwards.

I don't flirt, wear makeup or tight clothes to gain his attention.

In the back of her mind, she knew spazzing out on Ethan would get her arrested. She felt stranded and wanted to tell Mrs. G, but dreaded her reaction. It was her word against his and he sustained the operation. Making claims without evidence guaranteed a sunset eviction.

Life isn't fair.

She'd been assured, her living arrangement was secure, but *Ethan* changed the rules. He desired to *"know"* her biblically. She wasn't oblivious to his entrapment, and Tina must've seen them too.

My next move has to be considered, carefully.

She stared at the house across the street.

When I react emotionally, things never go as planned.

Running away used to be her method of exacting revenge…testing limits…bucking authority—however she justified it at the time. Even if she only inconvenienced Merle—*mission accomplished!*

This go round, *snatching independence*, hadn't panned out as envisioned.

I don't hate Stepping Stones.

What I regret is— jumping from a frying pan into a smoking oven!

KD would be out until ten, but she needed help now.

Her weed connect leaned against a phone booth at the top of the hill. When their eyes met, he smiled, and waved her over. She'd gone with her to cop enough times to feel safe seeing what he wanted. She also considered, *maybe he'll bless me with a blunt.*

"What up, lil mama."

"Hey, Dax."

"Why are you looking all mad?"

"I gotta get out of Stepping Stones. Mr. Franks, the house manager, is the worse."

"Is that where y'all stay? Didn't know. What did he do?"

"He's being a real jerk."

"If it's that bad—bounce."

"I feel you. I didn't wanna hurt my chances in court, but now that that's done..."

"Ah, shit! Court? Don't let me find out you're a trouble maker."

"Nah. It's nothing like that at all. Family stuff. Took care of it this morning. I's free."

"That's a good thing, right?"

"I'm realizing it's both a gift, and a curse."

"So what's the issue with where you live?"

"The people who run it are now saying I gotta pay rent."

"How much?"

"I didn't ask. Whatever it is it's too much. I more so hate that he even came at me the way he did?"

"I feel you, but you can't live anywhere for free."

"That's well and good, but Ethan Franks—he ain't right."

"You want me to send some goons for him?"

"Nah. Not yet." She smiled. "I'm just a little stressed. A lot has happen over the last couple of days."

"Can't let stress get the best of you."

"Who are you telling? I'm trying. Got any cheeba? A nick would set me straight."

"You know I do. It's time for a smoke break, anyway. You tryna roll with me? We can go up my cousin's spot. I bet nobody's there."

In the past, Dax only stared. She guessed he liked her, but one-on-one interactions with cute boys, had been rare.

"Aiight. No funny business. Just smoking."

"Cool—follow me."

11

DAX

"Where are we going?" JoJo didn't break stride.

Dax pointed to a weather-beaten two story clapboard at the end of the street. "It's right over there."

She slowed. "Hold up! Really?"

Sensing her disappointment, he grabbed her hand. "Come on. Next time, we'll go someplace better."

"Okay. I'm with you." *Next time? Hmmm.* It was broad daylight but the backdrop was still eerie. As they continued, she prayed, *Lord, be with me.*

Once a jewel, the house had fallen into disrepair. Most of the original details were intact, but it would take a lot of elbow grease to restore the glory. Save for a pathway to the door, water logged furniture, old car parts, and debris covered every inch of the porch. He reached between flowerpots for a tattered Pringles can and pulled out a ring of keys.

They stepped inside and the stink of stale cigarettes whacked them.

"Sit anywhere. Looks like we're alone after all. Make yourself at home. I'll turn on the AC. You thirsty?"

"A little."

"Bet. I'll see what their workin' with. Be right back."

She sat on the couch and looked around. A cloud of dust irritated her eyes, and triggered a fit of coughs. Atop the coffee table was a large ashtray filled to the brim with gray specks, brown seeds, smashed butts, and hundreds of green leaf roaches. She'd never seen anything like it. He returned with two glasses of grape soda, handed her one then began sifting through the pile. After finding a decent specimen, he sparked and hit it a few times, before passing it.

"Nah. Do you. Give me a bag and a blunt. I'll roll a new one." KD always said, "*Only blaze if you watch em roll up.*"

"Cool, cool, cool." He grinned, aware of the rule. He put two bright green nuggets on top of a magazine. "Can you roll?"

"Can I roll? *Hmmph!* Let's see."

She took her time breaking the weed into little bits, split the L, dumped the guts, filled the wrap, folded, rolled, licked, sealed, and admired it before lighting it. She sputtered. "*Whoa—this is strong.*"

"I'm glad you like it. I should have warned you bout that bud. I only blow the best."

She took a few more pulls before passing.

He inspected it. "You've got skills...roll betta than a lot of niggas. And you don't have a wet mouth. I'll get high with you anytime."

"Sounds good."

"So Miss JoJo... you have a man? And if not, why?"

"Well, mister...please, tell me you have a real name. I hate calling you Dax. It sounds so hood."

He chuckled. It had been so long since anyone had asked him his given name. "Derek."

"Hi Derek, I'm Joanna. It's nice to make your acquaintance."

"*Jo–ah- nah*—beautiful name. Nice to finally meet you too."

"Now, back to your question....to be honest with you...I've always been that girl that guys overlooked. I mean...I'd love a boyfriend. It just hasn't happen."

"Yeah—I hear that." He picked up the remote and turned on the TV. "You mind if I sit with you."

"Sure. This is your place."

She concealed it well, but he could see she was nervous. He smiled then sat at the other end of the chair. She was very attractive, but attacking wasn't his style. *There's time.*

"I see you looking all uptight. You're cool. I ain't gonna bite."

She felt silly. The weed was making her noid.

He flicked through the channels. "Anything you want to see?"

He'd already passed many of her favorites. "What about Tales from the Crypt? Go back a few clicks."

"You like horror movies, you know how to roll, you sexy, and brainy. Damn. Either niggas blind or you were made for me."

JoJo was speechless, still hung up on *"sexy."* She wished he'd say it again. *"Oh!"* she shouted. "Go back…back… yes! Have you ever seen this?"

"Nah."

"Well, it looks like it just started. You're gonna love the main character. Aw man! Just wait until his hair turns white. Then, it's on."

He wished she hadn't swerved his compliment, but her set up for the movie intrigued him. "What's it called?"

"Born Invincible."

"Aiight! So you gonna chill, and check out the flick, right?"

"Why not!" Curfew was at nine p.m. she had five hours to relax. She loved the direction, her day had turned. She anticipated trouble for not signing out, but decided to worry later.

"You've got me wanting to watch. Hungry? I can have it delivered."

"I'll eat some of yours."

"Nah…I already know. Chicks can eat. I'll get you whatever you want."

She bashfully grinned. "Let me see a menu."

He called in the order and they got comfortable while they waited. The more they talked, the more she realized she'd pegged him all wrong. He was intelligent, considerate of her feelings, witty and sweeter than she knew boys could be. She'd found him cute from day one, but expected he wouldn't be interested in a *Plain Jane*.

Throughout the afternoon, they ate, and watched a few movies. While super attentive, he never made her squirm. Hours later, his *"sexy"* comment still enthralled her. She couldn't stop thinking about his intentions.

"Derek—I hope you don't mind me calling you that."

"Only when we're alone."

"I promise." Without thinking of the implications, she blurted out, "I think I like you."

"Is that right? I think I like you too." Hearing her say it made him happy. "Why are you all the way over there? Mind if I get a little closer?"

"Yeah. I mean, no."

He moved nearer, and planted several soft kisses on her lips.

She smiled and asked him, "What do you like about me?"

"Your eyes, your height, and now, your sense of humor. I also like how your eyebrows arch when you're surprised."

"I see. Can you kiss me again?"

"Yes."

She didn't want the warm feeling to end. His lips were supple and soft.

With her firmly in his arms, he closed his eyes and stuck his tongue into her mouth. Certain he caught her by surprise, he proceeded slowly, until her strokes, matched his stride.

When Dax finally pulled away, he was breathless. "JoJo, I want you."

"I see." Pointing to his erection.

"Ignore that. He has a mind of his own."

Her eyes twinkled.

"I'm feeling your whole aura. You're different from the rest of these girls out here. There's something wholesome about you."

"Are you being for real? Wholesome?"

"Hell yeah! No bull. I can tell you're a good girl. I've been wanting to get with you, but didn't know how to approach you."

"You say that like you never see me."

"I see you, but it's never been the right time. I'm glad today happen. Spending time with you has been great. I haven't felt this way in a while."

"Me too…to all your points."

He put his arm around her and they kicked back. With both of their cards on the table, her comfort level increased. They kissed more before a booming system stopped in the front of the house.

"That's my cousin Tank and his girls. This should be a trip."

His girls (plural)?

The music stopped and a few minutes later, a man and woman entered in an uproar. Another, with a sheepish expression, came in behind them, and locked the door.

The one who'd been fussing, went upstairs. The other sat opposite of JoJo on the couch. She could feel the mute stranger's eyes on her from time to time, but didn't turn her head. Both reacted to a few of the same jokes, but that was the extent of their engagement.

"What up, cuz!"

"Same shit. What's new with you?" asked Tank before bopping into the kitchen, and opening the fridge. Dax followed, and watched him toss back a 40 of Mickey's.

"You good?"

"Yeah, I'm jiggy. I swear, if I ain't know better I'd think that bitch Chanel is stealing from me."

"Why you say that?"

"I don't question my gut. I don't wanna do it, but I'm gonna have to beat that hoe up. I know it. She likes talkin' out the side of her neck….being disrespectful. Can't let these hoes think they run shit."

"Chill, man. You start drinking and thinking crazy. Talk to her."

"I'ma talk to her all right. If you could've heard how she talked to me on the ride back from the sto. She betta thank God y'all was here, for real."

"*Chiiill*, yo. I don't want you running her off. Be nice."

He cracked open beer number two, swallowed a mouthful then burped. "I'll be nice. She looks stuck up…bourgeoisie, if you ask me. What's your angle? I've never known you to like challenges. The librarian-types don't make it easy to get the coochie."

"It's not like that. She's sweet. I like her a lot. Come on, let me introduce y'all."

Tank stood in front of Roxi, blocking her view of the TV. "Did you even speak?"

She pouted, and threw up her hands in frustration. "You told me to be quiet. I don't want any shit out of you."

"That's dumb, but I'm glad to know you listen to a nigga. Try doing it more. And don't be looking at me like that!"

"Like what? I made eye contact with you."

"Well, don't do that."

She craned her neck around him, and resumed watching the show.

"Wassup, Miss Lil No Peep?"

JoJo pointed to herself. "Who…. me?"

"You're the only stranger in the room." He held out his fist for her to give him a pound. She touched hers to his, but didn't like his energy. He undressed her with his beady eyes. His pink and black lips grossed her out. So not to fixate on them, she looked at Dax.

He grabbed her wrist. "This is JoJo. She's gonna be my girl."

Under different circumstances, the vow would've made her heart soar. After witnessing the cousin with "*his girls*," she was unsure.

"Oh, yeah? I'm happy for y'all."

12

DECISIONS, DECISIONS

*A*s JoJo flicked through the channels, she reminisced on her last encounter with Dax. She'd fallen hard and fast in love within a matter of weeks. The promise, *"I'll never leave you alone,"* made her put down her guard. While conventionally unwise, letting go was an exhilarating feeling.

He wanted to know everything about her—places she *"wanted to go,"* whether she wanted to *"live in the suburbs, boondocks or city,"* activities that *"made her happiest,"* and her views on *"World Peace."*

"Shower Me with Your love" was their song, both reviled Halloween, neither had ever owned a pet, and he conceded, *"Coming to America"* was a classic.

"I'm obsessed with your skin, your brown eyes with flecks of gold, you slim thick which I like and you're the right height. But the best of all is this baby mole on your cheek."

JoJo, loved his attention to detail. *"What about this hair that grows like a weed. Or these eyebrows that fight in the middle?"*

He didn't care about any of that. She enchanted him. *"I would love for our daughter to come out looking like you. You may not know your dad, but it's not because your mama was a whore. Lots of people can't say they've met the nigga. From what you've told me, your parents adored one another. You were born out of love. If you felt like you weren't before…those days are behind you. You are wanted. I will always be here for you. Baby—I want you."*

Dax also told her time would soften her hatred for her

grandmother. *"I've seen stranger things happen."* She'd been reluctant to talk about her past, and how she landed at the group home. Instead of mocking, he encouraged her to accept the things that shamed her, and to grow from her pain.

She couldn't imagine living without his love and hoped his feelings never changed. He begged her to trust him. Unlike his *cornball* cousin or the cruel boys from school, he was mature, kind and sensitive.

"You need me as much as I need you. There's just us."

Whenever they were alone, they lost track of time. On many nights, she put off going home until the last minute. Leaving his bed to battle the cold was getting old. They always said their final farewell at the top of the hill, where he stayed until she flicked the porch light.

Spending time with *her baby* and abiding by the curfew were real challenges. Mrs. G was back. *Ethan* stopped hounding her, but now—he monitored her "check-ins" and "outs," and punished her for the slightest mistake. She decided against telling Dax the full extent of her plight. He'd want to fight.

It was important she follow the rules for the next few weeks. Her seventeenth birthday was coming up. She couldn't spend it on lock.

JoJo heard KD enter the house, so she turned off the TV and followed. She stomped into her room without knocking, and sat on the bed. "One week!" Saying the period of penance aloud pissed her off again.

"A whole week? For being five minutes late? He's playing a bunch of games."

"Who you telling? He says, I think I'm above the law."

"Whatever that means. Mr. Franks got a hankering for some fresh booty and you're not giving it up. Chile, you better quit being selfish."

"Gross! You joke entirely too much."

"All jokes aside, what are you going to do?"

"For now, nothing. He has me jammed up. But rest assured,

Ethan will get his."

KD agreed. "Every dog has his day."

"*I knooow.* It's so not fair."

"Life rarely is."

She smiled through gritted teeth. "I'm so damn mad. What is it about me?"

"I can't answer that, but I must ask—why were you late? You've signed out a lot lately. Wassup with that?"

JoJo pointed to the wall behind her. "*Ooh,* is this a new poster?"

"Nah—don't changed the subject. Spill it."

"I have a boyfriend."

"A who? You've been holding out on me. I swear, I thought we were better than that."

"We are. It happened, unexpectedly."

"Well, I'll be." KD shook her head, surprised she'd hadn't a clue. "Congrats, homie. I'm happy for you. So, when do I get to size him up?"

"You already have," said JoJo under her breath.

"What was that? Speak up."

"You know him."

"Who?"

"Don't judge me."

"Who?"

"Dax."

"Really! Got to admit—I wasn't expecting that. Interesting. You like them pretty."

"Pretty?" She repeated the typically feminine descriptor for confirmation.

"Yes….he's a looker. I can see why girls like him."

"What does that mean? I assumed y'all were cool."

"He's cool. I'm cool. We're cool. He keeps decent greenery, but I don't sit around shootin' the boh boh wit the nigga. Mixing business with pleasure, ain't my thing."

KD's statement stung. "Well, he treats me nice and we have a lot in common."

"As I said, before I even knew it was him, I'm happy for you. Come on—what you eat don't make me shit."

"*Eww*—you're so crass."

"Why, thank you."

"And regarding your statement, 'you can see why a girl would like him'. What do you like in a guy?"

"Nothing."

"You like girls?"

"Yes."

"You're gay? I can't believe I never knew." A trillion salacious questions came to mind, but JoJo refrained for fear of making her uneasy. "How long have you known?"

"I'd say, since I was twelve."

"Have you ever had a boyfriend?"

"No, and I'm still a virgin, but I know what I like."

"I see." JoJo looked confused. She didn't understand how one could swear off the opposite sex, but respected her decision.

KD laughed. "It's not complicated unless you wanna make it. Any who—I need to get out of here. Got a promotion last week. I'm now the unit supervisor. If you want, I can get you a gig."

"I'll think about it. Thanks for offering."

"No doubt." She affixed a laminated badge to her shirt and grabbed her steel toe boots. "Will I see you later?"

"Yeah. Where else I'ma be? Wait. Let me answer that. I'll be on the couch, with Jeremy, watching TV."

"That's funny, actually. I'm sure he'll be happy to see you."

"Lovely."

"I don't know about you sometimes. Trouble is your pal. Till this day— you still the only person I ever met who ran away from a mansion."

As if I need a reminder. "You wouldn't understand."

"You're probably right. I've gotta get out of here. I'll see ya later."

"Deuces."

KD left knowing they saw eye to eye on few things, but their friendship meant more to her than gold. No matter the fallout from her poor decisions, she'd be there to bring JoJo in from the cold.

The last place she ever expected to be was a home for wayward minors. Two summers before, she and *Pops* sailed along the *Gulf of Mexico* from *Tampa* to *Corpus Christi*. From there, they trekked West over the road. In San Jose, they lowered the top on the rented Thunderbird and raced up the seaboard. The combined twenty-seven hundred miles was long and tiring, but every day was eventful. They stopped in a new city each night, slept in five-star hotels, and dined with silverware, candles and white linens. Her eyes to misted, as she recalled forgotten facets of the trip.

Photos from their *"fantastic voyage"* covered the wall over her bed. She'd felt little joy since the day she discovered him dead. KD hadn't realized until then how much their last vacation meant.

Before her arrival, KD stayed with Apostolics who swore she was hell bound without repentance. At the time, sexuality was the furthest thing from her mind. They took one look at her, labeled her a heathen and withheld the protection and direction they signed on to provide.

At *Stepping Stones,* she found acceptance. Mrs. Grant said she wanted her to succeed, and hadn't broken her promises. A schoolmate of hers, Alderman Brock, enrolled her in a skills development program run by the district. Unlike others her age, she had long term goals and ambitions.

She didn't possess JoJo's natural beauty, slim figure, and intellect. All of her achievements came from hard work, and focus on the future. Life wasn't fair, and she was a black girl aware of how little time she had to waste. *Eighteen will be here before I know it.*

JoJo entered her room. Oddly, Ramona wasn't there. She retrieved *Charlene* and a notebook from the dresser, then sat at her desk.

Punishment separates me from Dax.

This time it's seven days, but the next time it could be more.

That would be torture!

KD could only give her but so much useful advice. She'd never laid with a man. *Once a girl does, nothing's ever the same.*

Until now, orgasms came from self-stimulation. Masturbating since nine, she knew the right tugs and swipes to reach a delicious conclusion. Making love to Dax felt like a christening. The spasms she experienced, at the tip of his dick, were prolonged and dizzying. There was no pain, guilt, pressure, nor fear of rejection. Not once, did she question her worthiness for the enchanted feeling. She let down her guard, and didn't regret it.

While walking her home, they weighed an option she hadn't considered. *"I was thinking—I might as well move over here. I already talked to my people. I spend a lot on cabs, coming back and forth each day. I'd rather spend that money on you. If you want—you can stay with me. It's a family house. He can't tell me no."*

"That would be amazing. I mean your cousin is a little off, but I'll manage with you by my side."

"Don't worry about him. I love my cousin and yeah that nigga talk a lot of shit, but he don't want me to box his ass up. He might be older, but I've always been the one with the hands."

His proposal was enticing, but going AWOL from *Stepping Stones* meant no turning back.

He stopped her under the street light, squeezed her ass and kissed her. *"I don't know what it is about you. You make me feel—different."*

"How so?"

"Before I knew you…when I'd see you with KD, I thought you were fine. But now—man, I look at females totally different. That's if I notice them at all. You're not like the rest of these dumb birds out here."

"You're such a sweetheart. As for being smart–I was taught to think critically. I found you intimidating, but cute too. In case you didn't notice, I'm sorta shy. I'm glad you decided to act on your attraction."

"Of course. I was waiting until I caught you alone."

"Oh really?"

"Hell yeah. JoJo, you've given me a whole new motivation. Ya know—I never imagined it happening to me."

After the accolades, his hand wringing was confusing. *"What happened?"*

"You want me to say it?"

"Yes—please."

"Joanna, I love you. I wanna be with you forever. My parents have been married over twenty years. I want the same for us. You're a flower who deserves to be watered, nurtured, and protected."

"I love you too and I want the same. Hearing you say it, means everything."

After replaying the conversation in her head, then weighing the risks, and rewards of following his course, she grabbed her backpack, and prepared for the move.

13

CROSSROADS

Within a month, JoJo settled into her new digs. Dax bought pillows, the bed-in-a-bag she wanted and a thirty-two-inch color TV. They talked about installing a private line so she could stay in touch with KD. She learned to make grits, eggs, bacon and toast the way he liked them. Other than that, he cooked or they ordered out.

The house was larger than it appeared. There were three bedrooms on the second level, and a basement with a low ceiling. The spigot in the adjacent bathroom constantly dripped, but being together made the annoyance worth it. Until they could get their own, they transformed their portion into a palace.

Deserting *Stepping Stones* meant dependence on Dax, but he never bitched or moaned. Instead of rubbing it in her face, he spoiled her. Since he sorted the mail, she assumed any money Merle sent, went to Mr. Franks. If she didn't dread losing the peace she'd obtained, she'd call, and request she stop paying.

She'd teetered on leaving for days when he forced her out the door.

After firmly rebuffing his advances, he turned cold. Late one night, he pinned her in the office and presented two options—*"give up the twat or you're on your own!"*

So far, she was happy with her choice.

Managing money came naturally. Even when she had access to expense accounts and credit cards, spending never gave her a rush. As long as she had the basics, she didn't want for much else.

During the day, she shopped or went to the library to kill time. Until their living situation stabilized, college would wait. Studying would be impossible with the schedule and fickle temperaments of their roommates. Plus, she didn't want to choose a major, she'd end up hating. She considered getting a job, but Dax always told her, *"Let's talk about that later."*

It didn't take much time to realize Chanel and Roxi were different breeds. Weighing only a hundred and ten pounds wet, Roxi was more adorable than alluring. Her light complexion, sandy brown hair, and freckles, attracted those who preferred their fun *"young."* On the timid side and sweet; the teen had been the easiest to engage. The older, classier of the two, Chanel, didn't say much to anyone. Usually, she grabbed a plate from the kitchen, and went up to her room. She was a Wu-Tang Clan super fan. Mentioning *"Method Man"* was the first time JoJo saw her smile.

One day, Tank was in love, the next he despised them both. He belittled and talked shit about them while totaling the dollars each earned. Neither complained.

How can women lie with him, sing his name, then suck and buck, for his gain?

She questioned whether he cared for them at all. He never showed love. Day in and day out, he fussed, cursed, and acted tough. Hardworking, but not respected for their grind—*life for a shorty shouldn't be so rough.*

Dax was his polar opposite, and she revered him for it. Calm, measured and considerate. He introduced her to new things daily, never compromised her morals or forced her to do anything belittling. When he came in the house at night, he turned off the pager. In a selfish world, he carved out time to love on her. No one had ever done that before.

Sitting with him while he *"bagged up the work"* became their tradition. The time-consuming process gave them time to discuss the past, present and future.

From the descriptions of his squad, fights stories, running game, and the shame of befriending lames, she learned he wasn't a *"yes"* man, and didn't take shit from anyone. He never shielded her from the rewards, hazards, and horrors of hustling. Everything she knew about the game, came from his play book.

She worried when he was in the streets, but she reasoned— *No body dies over a trees.*

Early on, smoke in the air—24/7, caused her to stress over minor things, and ask lots of questions. She knew it killed his buzz, but he kept it to himself.

Other than weed, Dax had few other vices, except for looking good. At least twice a week, JoJo headed to PG Plaza to pick up a pair of *"zooms."* She didn't mind the trips. Bus and train rides were relaxing. He always knew what he wanted, and called ahead to make sure his selections were waiting behind the counter.

"Boy, you sure love the color blue."

"I've been told it looks good on me. It's my dad's favorite color too. They say, when he was my age, he had more swagger than sense."

"Well, since we're talking sense—why do you have two pairs of the same shoes?"

"When I find something I like, I cop one to rock, and one for stock."

She ran her hand across the items she'd hung in the closet. Arranged by color, with the hangers facing the same direction, his wardrobe resembled a rack in a swank boutique. His footwear, dress shirts, slacks, and neckties, formed symmetrical ombre-colored rows. It was one of the ways he reminded her of Franklin. Both, loved looking impeccable.

"I wanna take you out."

JoJo spun around and excitedly asked, "Where?" He rarely proposed going out.

Once, they rode the Metro to Union Station, lunched at

Bojangles' and caught a movie. It was the first outing both considered a date. Before hopping back on the train, they stopped at a gelato shop in the atrium and shared a butterscotch sundae. They lovingly walked, hand in hand. Stares from other women were flattering. Dax was certified Grade A fine, and by some twist of fate, she was the apple of his eye.

"Oh, I don't know–maybe to dinner, then the Crossroads."

"*Ooh!* That sounds fun." She'd heard about the hotspot on the radio. Then, her own words came back to haunt her—*those dresses and frilly shit can stay.*

"I'd love to go to dinner, but the club? I don't know. I have nothing to wear."

"Clothes? Come here… set the rest of that stuff on the hamper. We can deal with that later. Sit your fine ass down, on daddy's lap."

She complied. "Okay, daddy."

He grabbed her chin, and aligned their eyes. "I love everything about you. Your beauty marks, and your flaws."

"Flaws?"

"From the way you bite your lip when you think, to that little mole under your left eye. Please don't take my comment the wrong way. Shit's sexy."

"Okay."

"I'm going to put you on the pedestal you deserve. Nothing but the best for you. Just give me a little time. You deserve it all. We're up out of here, in a couple of months. I'll get us a spot with a nice kitchen, big windows, and a walk-in for your stuff alone. You hear me?"

"Yes."

"Keep being as sweet as you are. Keep loving me. I got us. As for not having something to wear tonight."

"Tonight?"

"Yes–but for now, let's smoke a ribbean of this dozier I've been holding. After that, hopefully, you'll give me some booty. We can go to the mall when we wake up?"

"Wake up? You plan to put it down like that?"

"Hell yeah."

"Okay!"

He kissed her. "I know we can find you something real sexy. Tank will get Roxi to hook your hair up."

"Don't worry, we're cool. I'll ask her."

"All right! Now, that we have that out the way, you should lay back for a second."

"For what?" She grinned at him mischievously. "I thought you were tryna smoke again."

"*Mmmm*, I've already got the muchies."

Dax ran with a group of guys from various parts of PG County. They drove flashy cars—fast, and always blasted Go-go and Southern rap. Regal, a short, loud mouth with a black Buick Regal, was his best friend, and their driver for the evening.

When he and JoJo climbed inside, they bid the couple upfront a "*good evening*," but only Regal returned the greeting. "*Kema*", riding shotgun, toyed with her long braids, never acknowledged their presence. The dark tints, leather seats, and AC made for a smooth ride. They kissed, and cuddled the entire time, unaware of their antisocial car mates.

It took twenty minutes to make their way through the roped aisles to the entrance. Captivated by the sights around her, JoJo didn't notice the time. People of all hues, draped in showy couture, stood in front and behind them, amped to join the pandemonium.

JoJo had no problem using the fake ID, she'd had for years. The bouncer barely looked up, while waving them through the turnstile.

After paying, the pairs made a beeline for the bar.

"I'm gonna see about getting us one of those high tops." Regal pushed through the throng.

Dax pulled her to the side. "I'll grab us drinks."

The girls didn't talk while waiting for the boys to return. Kema's posture, and pursed lips were a cold shoulder, but JoJo found her haughtiness amusing. She was a model-type, who looked mixed with black and Oriental. Her doe eyes, long face, and seductive gait, gave her gazelle-like grace. Her outfit was designer, and her rounded nails were French-tipped. She appeared out of her date's league, but only *they* knew the terms of their arrangement.

Concern for their affair disappeared when Dax squeezed her hand. She peeped Kema's mug and thought, *she doesn't like Regal at all.*

Once seated, they ordered a platter of jerk wings and crispy plantains to share. After washing it down with another drink, Dax asked her to dance.

"You see these things. I have two left feet."

"Kill that noise. Can't fool me. We know you can move that body."

She blushed.

"Be yourself! You don't know these people. Who cares what they think. The only opinions that matter are ours." He scanned the room until he spotted someone illustrating his point. "Look… look at that clown over there."

She located the source of his amusement. "Unc gettin' down. Oh shit—was that a handstand?"

"I think you have to get up on both hands for it to count."

"Right!" He grabbed her hand.

"O-kay. I'll go, but I've warned you."

"I'll take my chances. Rege, y'all coolio?"

He looked at Kema. She looked away. "Yeah, man. Do your thing."

Dancehall entranced the floor, and stirred the revelers into a frenzy. As if the *"intrinsic riddims"* weren't enough, foot-stomping and wall-banging, amplified the vibration.

The Long Island Ice Teas she'd downed relaxed her limbs, and lessened her mortification. It only took a few songs to adjust to the tempo, and her partner's gyrations. Soon, she found herself enjoying the deed more than she imagined possible. Loose, but still in control, when she wobbled, he caught her.

Gazing into his hazel eyes, she felt like the luckiest girl in the world.

Under the strobes, Dax looked spectacular. Numerous chicks tried to gain his attention, but he acted like he didn't know them. Emboldened by his pride, she leaned in, and kissed him.

Her nerve shocked him, but he'd never front.

He responded, without concern for who observed the stunt.

"Was that a test?"

"No. I was just saying thank you for the date."

He pulled a napkin from his pocket and patted her forehead. "You're welcome. Let's take a break."

"Y'all ready?" asked Regal, interrupting their moment. He'd been watching them since the prior song.

"What's wrong?" Dax didn't like the look on his face.

"Nothing."

"Aiight, Moe. We're ready." Realizing the fourth in their party was gone, he asked, "What happened?"

"It don't even matter. Can't control no hoe."

As they exited the club, JoJo noticed Kema climbing into a black Corvette. "Where's she going?"

"Fuck that bitch!" Regal didn't look back. When they reached his car, he pulled a bottle of liquid from his boot and shook it. "Y'all wanna roll up?"

"Hell no!" Dax's eyes narrowed to slits.

"Okay, okay. Just asking. I'll put it away."

"Come on, nigga. Open up!"

Regal got in, and started the engine. After opening JoJo's door, he reclined in the passenger seat.

"All right. All right! What y'all tryna do? It's still early, and I'm not ready to call it a night."

Dax looked back at her. "Dippers or wet—stay away from that shit, baby. No matter what anybody say. I saw a woman strip butt naked, and run up and down the street off one hit." He pointed to his friend. "This nigga lunchin."

JoJo was only interested in normal, organic bud—the kind she could break apart, sift through, and toss out the seeds. "I get it, baby. No thank you."

"Good."

"Can we go to the Pancake House?"

He bobbed his head, embracing the idea. "You want some panny cakes?

"Yes, please"

"I could eat. I haven't had steak and eggs in a while. Cool. Stacks—it is!" He looked at Regal, but didn't speak. Feeling the heat, he peeled off.

Stacks served as a meeting place for D.C.'s Black residents since the 1970s. During an earlier era, numerous Civil Rights Movement sit-ins were staged at the long counter. The menu, like the wall-to-wall stainless steel and yellow and white art deco booths, had changed little over the years. Silk carnations, in porcelain vases, still topped the tables, and washed-out headshots, lined the otherwise sparsely decorated walls.

Few luminaries visited these days, but the diner remained an around the clock attraction. The grub was secondary to being spotted inside the institution. Often, what began on one of the city's many dance floors, continued under fluorescent lights surrounded by the aroma of swine.

On Friday and Saturday nights, rap music pumped from in-ceiling speakers, and the chain-smoking waitresses were more likely to cuss you out than properly greet you.

They arrived at 2:30 a.m., and had to wait in line. The dessert case, filled with homemade cakes, pies, and pastries provoked their hungry eyes.

"Your sandals are nice." A third girl told JoJo that evening. She smiled politely. Though her feet throbbed, she'd never felt so pretty. She would've never selected a short dress or peep-toe, but Dax won her over. *"You have the shape of men's dreams."*

The tabletop jukebox should've been in a museum. Astonished it worked, JoJo played a few tunes. The fellas talked quietly about their need for "loot."

Their meals arrived as six guys entered, and ambled through a sea of annoyed faces. A hostess trailed behind with menus as bussers hurried to connect tables in the section marked "Closed for Cleaning."

JoJo whispered to her companions. "Must be nice."

Regal never shifted his gaze. "Yeah–that's how they treat ballers."

Though blinged out and dressed-to-impress, none had her baby's glow. "Is that what that is? *Humph*! From the looks of things, they brought out the Gucci store."

Dax wiped his mouth, and tossed his napkin on the table. He didn't comment on the display, but cogs turned in his brain. "What about those Skins?"

"It's our year!"

"Josey, I'm gonna call a taxi to come take you back to the crib."

"Why? Did I do something wrong?"

"Hell no. Tonight's been all that. You look amazing. Smell amazing." He got closer. "I'm sure you taste amazing too. I can't wait to find out."

JoJo covered her mouth with her hand and smiled. She loved when he talked dirty, and hoped he never stopped.

"I'm glad we did this."

"Me too."

"You had a good time, right?"

"The best."

"We have to go out again—soon."

"I agree, anytime."

"Sit tight. Me and Rege finna step outside. Grab the check for me."

"Okay."

It saddened her the night was ending, but the *"itus"* had kicked in. She only wished he were leaving too.

Dax settled the bill, and the threesome stepped into the pre-dawn air. They weren't there long when a yellow cab stopped. Dax opened the back door. JoJo got inside. He handed her a twenty before leaning in for a lingering kiss. "I'll be home in a bit."

"Fine. Bye."

"Never that. We don't say bye. How does, us staying in all day, sound?"

"You're not being fair. I love cuddling."

"I always play fair with you. I'll see you soon!"

After losing the battle with a yawn, she relented. "Okay. Hurry up, and come get in the bed with me."

"I love you, baby. Put on some thongs." He shut the door.

She shouted through the window. "I will, and I love you too."

The taxi pulled off.

She waved until he was out of view.

14

MOURNING

BOOM!

A loud bang jolted JoJo awake. She sat up, and reached for Dax. He wasn't there. In fact, he'd never touched his side of the bed.

To her horror, Tank stood in the doorway gripping his crotch. Making matters worse, her nipples were poking through the thin beater she'd worn to be sexy. She pulled the blanket up to her neck. "What's your problem?"

"You need to come down stairs."

"Why? What do you want?"

"We got on the news, and it looks like your boyfriend's got himself into a pickle."

"What's a pickle?"

Tank laughed. "Come on which yo green ass, and see for yourself. Chanel called me hoopin' and hollerin' about a robbery at a hotel in Cheverly. I missed it the first time, but I waited for a spell. At the top of the hour—*sho nuff*—there he was. Looking like uncle Bug. Dat nigga mugshot came up on the screen, and I almost spilled my drank."

She screamed. "Noooooo! Okay—I'm coming. Let me put on some clothes. Can you close the door behind you?"

He swung it open and close, a few times. "You really want me to leave?"

"What do you mean? Do I want you to leave? Hell yeah. Get the hell outta here. You know good and well Dax wouldn't

76

appreciate you bussin' up in here on me like you did. I'm damn near naked."

His appraisal felt disgusting. She prayed he left, without interruption.

"*Mmmmh*—I didn't know." He backed out the room, but left the door open.

She put on a bra, donned sweatpants, a big t shirt, and flip flops then headed to the living room. After listening to the story on numerous stations, she was shocked and dismayed to learn, Tank's account was true.

Back in their room, she balled up in a fetal position, and cried for over an hour. Afterwards, she got into bed, pulled the covers up to her neck, and thought about the prior night.

He'd been more preoccupied than usual, but I figured he was planning something big. Shit! I thought our night on the town was a celebration. Then, there was his reaction to the guys in the pancake house. Dax, with nothing to say—yeah, that was weird. What did you and Regal do?

When Tank and the girls left a few hours later, she showered, put the same sweats back on, and fashioned her hair in two braids. If there was anything of value in the room, she wanted to find it first.

She stripped the bed, alphabetized their CDs, and cleaned off the dresser tops with a damp rag. Still antsy, she went through his belongings. Several hours later, in a gym bag stuffed in the back of the closet, she discovered thirteen hundred dollars, and a Zip Lock freezer bag full of weed.

Elated, she disrobed for bed, contemplating where to hide the cash and drugs. *Behind a dresser, in the pockets of Dax's folded jeans, in the ceiling? None of those will do. Until she figured out a solution, staying close to the house appeared the best move.*

His call or letter, were her only concerns.

Come on, baby. Call me. Call, your girl.

15

F*CK ME— NO! F*CK YOU

A week and a half passed without word from Dax. Not knowing what he faced, made it hard for JoJo to sleep and think. Smoking helped in the past, but these days, gave her migraines.

Their *"sanctuary of serenity"* became a prison of memories. Every time the phone rang and it wasn't him, her heart sunk lower. Writing letters kept her sane. *Once I get an address, I'll mail one, each day.* She had the money and grass, but neither fixed her fear of the unknown.

Stranded and defenseless once again!

In *Dax's* absence, she felt out of place. At any time, Tank could tell her to bounce. She could leave, but where would she go?

Back to Stepping Stones? Not an option, unless I give a dog a bone.

After the emancipation hearing, she never saw the therapist or Nancy Mallory again. Contacting the latter crossed her mind, but she worried about complicating her situation.

Tired of the stillness, but scared of venturing far, she humbly accepted, voluntary house arrest. Without a safe place to put her stash, she kept the money strapped to her waist and stored the weed in tampon boxes, she sat on the floor next to the dresser. While not the most secure location, it was uninteresting enough, to deter a moron like Tank.

Through the paper thin walls, she heard everything going on in the next room. Loud as a crowd, she wondered if he projected his voice on purpose. He'd reached his tipping point. The combination of *"stiff balls"* and zero *"new money"* were dissolving his fragile patience.

"I'm sorry Tank. Let me suck it, instead. If I don't do as the doctor instructed, I'll only prolong the infection."

JoJo was glad Chanel heeded the pharmacist's warning. "Abstinence is a must!"

"That shit ain't working fast enough!"

"It hurts. That's why I went to the pharmacy in the first place. I'd take it if they were gentle, but I can't tell a trick how to get his money's worth. I just need a couple more days. Then I'll be back to normal."

"Bitch, you laying around here all day not doing shit. Don't let that hussy in the next room get you fucked up!"

"That's unfair! I more than pull my weight."

"You've gotten lazy. Heating this house, and feeding y'all greedy asses ain't easy, either."

In the months JoJo had been around, Tank proved to be a belligerent drunk. When his mind was set, negotiations were over. As she continued listening, she feared where this was going.

"Stop, Tank! Stop it! Why are you doing this? Please stop!"

Then she heard a loud slap followed by silence.

"You can pass a yeast infection to someone else. I don't want Roxi to go through this too."

"I done smashed ten times since I last fucked you. And I don't use condoms with either of you."

"I figured as much. That's why I'm warning you."

"You in my bed. Got that ass sitting out like that! I want some."

"Dammit, Tank! Stop it!"

"Shut up!"

JoJo heard fabric ripping followed by, *"Ahhhh.* You're so warm. I love this shit. Yes!"

Yuck! JoJo felt sick.

"Bitch! What is all this white shit on my dick? Explain!"

"Fuck you!"

"Fuck me? Fuck me? No…no…fuck you. Lay back down. Fuck it. I'm in it now."

"Stop, Tank! Stop."

"Don't fight me!"

"Why won't you listen to me?"

"You know you love me. Take it!"

Chanel soon accepted her fate. "*Mmmh*. I hate that you're doing this. I can't stand you."

"Whatever. You love me."

The metal frame and mattress coils squeaked and hawed as he plowed her vagina full throttle. He grunted between pumps. "I missed this shit…Ooooh!"

His climax, made the mutts outback, bark and howl.

The snuffles, and teeth grinding that followed, prevented everyone, save him, from sleeping.

Instantly, JoJo's bed felt a million times emptier.

A woman had been raped, and she didn't move or utter a word.

She moaned like it felt good.

Besides, what was I supposed to do?

16

SAY A PRAYER

The clock radio read five a.m.

Dammit! These fools are at it again.

Since Dax's arrest, she'd gotten little sleep. Wide awake, she turned on the bedside lamp, and listened to the disharmony. The living room TV was on full blast, but did little to muffle screaming, and shattering glass.

I need another place to stay! The stress of being in the house was making her sick. Throughout the day, she popped Tums like candy. After a third week of uncertainty, she still couldn't eat or think.

Tank berated the girls the prior two days, and was drinking more than usual. The assault made Chanel's symptoms worse, which enraged him even more. A week off the street, turned into two. Roxi worked, but didn't hustle as hard as the veteran.

From upstairs, she heard him banging on his chest. "Fuck is you talkin too? I think you forgot who's running this show. I feed you bitches. Put clothes on your backs…point y'all in the right direction." Followed by, "Get off me Tank. You're hurting me" and screams.

She jumped out the bed, ran downstairs, and nearly tripped over Chanel. "What's going on?"

"Same o, same o!"

"Why are you sitting on the bottom step, in the dark? I thought I heard crying?"

"Shit ain't right. I don't know how much longer I can take it. That nigga, don't have no right, putting his hands on nobody."

JoJo had never seen her upset. The emotion was actually refreshing. "You're right! Why's he going in on Roxi? Where are they now?"

She pointed to the kitchen.

"Come with me."

"I can't get into that. And I don't suggest you to go in there, either."

"What do you mean?" JoJo pulled on her t-shirt.

"I don't want him mad at me too. He's an animal when he's drunk and stoned. I learned long ago, to stay out of other's affairs. He whipped my ass last night. Every inch of my body hurts."

Then there was a loud crash, which startled them both. Chanel didn't budge. *Scared Bitch! Lord give me the strength.*

Roxi laid unconscious in the corner. Before JoJo assessed her condition, a bottle flew towards her head. Seeing his hand movement, she spun, and avoided getting hit. Amber liquid covered the floor and walls. "Shit!"

"Mind your business, bitch! Your opinion ain't wanted on nuffin'. Don't you worry bout how me and my bitches get down. We did just fine before you arrived."

"I'm not worried. I just want to know—why were you in here hoopin and hollerin, and why is Roxi spread eagle?"

"We were talking about my money. Matter of fact—ain't nothing wrong with that puss of yours. I know that joint can take a hit. I've most definitely jerked off to Dax beating the breaks off of it."

"You's a nasty, drunk fucker."

"Whatever."

"Fuck you!"

"Fuck me? You're funny. I give you a place to lay your nappy head. You don't do shit for me. And I can show you better than I can tell you how nasty I am."

"Have you checked on her?"

"She's all right. And because you're running your mouth, I'm giving your ass a week to find some bread, or you're gonna have to roll, how we roll, round here. Cuzzo ain't here to float you." He wiggled his long snake of a tongue. Sweat dripped from his face.

"Whatever."

"I can dress you up, get Chanel to teach you how to walk in heels, and make that little ass of yours pop out."

"You must be confused. I didn't come in here for this. You need to stop hitting that girl. She can't take it. Can't you see that?"

"I don't see shit, but wasted potential."

"Check it—I will never be one of your girls. Get that out of your head."

"If you don't like my house—get out! I'm shich of yourship!" He became louder and more slurred with each syllable.

JoJo giggled to let him know she wasn't afraid. "I'm ship of yo witch! What the hell are you saying?" One swift kick could've knocked him out his shoes.

"You heard me!"

"You need to calm your ass down. Lay down. Go to bed."

"Don't tell me what to do."

No one noticed Roxi advance, looking demented, with a cast iron pan clasped between her hands. The overhand swing, and connecting blow to the dome, reverberated around the room. Tank frowned, grabbed his crown and leaned forward. As he fell to the floor, his head connected with the table's edge. For sixty seconds, everyone froze in shock.

JoJo clutched his wrist, and moved her fingers around in search of a pulse. "I think he's dead!"

"What are we gonna do? God help me. Look at him. What've I done?"

Chanel entered with a smirk. "What's done is done. Fuck him!"

"Don't say that. He's dead!" Roxi bawled. "What should I do? Who should we call? I don't wanna go to the electric chair."

She laughed. "Let me get this straight—this bastard would've killed you had JoJo not intervened, and you're worried bout him? You've got to be the silliest hoe I've ever met."

"He took care of us."

"No, bitch! We took care of him. And how did he repay us? Sell us for bargain basement prices? Put us out the car in the snow? Beat our asses? Tell us we ain't shit? Will I miss any of that? Let me think for a tick—Hell no! At the end of the day, some niggas gotta go. He was one of them."

"Wow. I feel sorry for you. Tank said, you wasn't loyal."

JoJo wished she could evaporate or, at a minimum, block out the babble. Since she could do neither, she meditated as Dr. McDowell had taught her—*One Mogadishu...Two Mogadishu... Three Mogadishu...Four.*

"Wow, my ass. You loved that nigga didn't you? Damn." Chanel glared at her oppressor's stiffening body. "And you're funny as shit. Don't feel sorry for me. Feel it for your damn self. He didn't give two shits about none of us. Loyal, to what?"

"We need to call the police."

"No the fuck we don't. Does our story make a lot of sense? Will they believe it was self-defense? Both of y'all are juveniles, and I'm sure there's a failure to appear warrant out for my arrest. Nine times out of ten, they're gonna send someone who's been here in the past. Last thing we need is anyone asking a bunch of questions."

JoJo thought, *what have I gotten myself into? How do I make these dumb bitches shut up?*

"Oh, you're right. But, maybe. I'm so confused. I can't handle pressure. I need a drink."

Chanel stormed to a cabinet on the other side of the kitchen. "A drink! A drink! You always need a damn drink." She retrieved a glass, slammed it on the counter and filled it halfway with Jack. The bottle top was still off from Tank's last pour. "Here."

With shaky hands, Roxi drained the content in one gulp. The spirit burned as it passed through her throat. No one understood the place he occupied in her heart. He'd been a merciless bastard, but he'd raised her. She loved him.

Despite being together, the girl's felt miles apart. For several minutes, each cried, on the inside.

After reaching a clearer mental space, JoJo asked, "Are you two finished yet?" Neither responded. "First, we're not calling anyone. I have an idea. Let's find shovels in the shed, and dig a hole. After that, we'll drag the body out back, and bury it. I don't wanna hear any objections. Nair one of you got a plan, and I have zero interest in prison."

Chanel scrutinized both for signs of wavering. "Fine by me. Sounds better than standing around looking dumb."

Work on the six-by-six foot pit (*give or take a few inches*) continued well into the afternoon. With each thrust of their tools, JoJo prayed they didn't hit a power line or big root. The distance between the houses shielded their work from peeping toms. Chanel bitched most, but ended up being a team player. Though banged up, Roxi did her part, without complaining.

A large tree with flowering foliage cloaked Tank's unmarked grave. The finished product wasn't as symmetrical as planned, but served their purpose. Afterwards, Roxi suggested a prayer.

Chanel jerked, and looked over her shoulder. "A what?"

"Everyone deserves one. It's the least we can do."

She turned to JoJo. "You hear this shit?"

Alarmed by her insensitivity, JoJo squeezed her shoulder. "Come on—let me talk to you." When they were out of earshot, she paused. "Lighten up. This clearly means a lot to her."

"Means a lot to Roxi? Ha! We worked like Hebrew slaves to clean up the mess she created. I'm hot. I'm hungry, and need a shower. Let's get the bastard in the ground. I'm already over this shit."

"I know, and I appreciate all you've done. For real. Just do this for me."

"I did what you asked of me, all day. Roxi's pathetic. I ain't never seen the bitch pray over a meal, but she wanna say a blessing for the devil? I can't support that. It's mind boggling to me. And let me tell you something—Tank lied. Dax called a few times. He told him, you packed your shit and left, after you heard his charges. He told us he'd beat our asses if we told you."

"Do you know anything about his case?"

"I'm sorry. I don't. For what it's worth, I think he really loves you."

"Let's get this over with. We still got to sprinkle a layer of that grass seed I saw out back. Then, we'll wipe down the kitchen. We should all put on rubber gloves. When we're done, I'll find us something to eat. Work with me, please. I'm running on gas fumes. Come on. Just hang in there a little longer."

Inside, she raged, glad Tank was dead.

The slime ball would've forced me to stroll in a matter of days.

The multitude of questions, she planned to ask, also raced through her brain.

"Okay, JoJo. I'll do you a solid. You know—I've got to give it to you. You're far from a fool. Tank pegged you all wrong. I didn't see you as the G, you've proven to be. I'll bow my head to make the cry baby happy, but my words won't be for him. They'll be for our health, wealth, and prosperity."

"Even better."

17

BEST FRIENDS

*J*oJo tossed pebbles at the ledge. "KD! *Pssst! Psssst!* Kaaaaay D!"

"Tap!... Tap!... Tap!"

She stepped back, and saw her girl standing in the window frame with a finger pressed to her lips. After a few seconds of fiddling with the old lock and sliding mechanism, she stuck her head through the opening.

"Bout damn time."

"Pipe down. What are you doing out here?"

"Come downstairs, and I'll explain."

"Come where? Are you faded?"

"Don't be a pussy, Kaori. I'll meet you out back."

Stepping Stones occupied a large American Four Square home with a wraparound porch. Doors led to the front, back yard, basement and a fire escape on the third floor. With know-how, one could easily make it in and out undetected. Certain floorboards creaked, but KD taught her to sneak. On countless nights, they'd tiptoed out for heart-to-hearts, or to smoke under the stars.

Ten minutes later, she exited the house, and whispered into the darkness. "Where are you at?"

"Over here."

KD ducked under the Willow's limbs, and joined JoJo on the bench. "It's cold out here. I should've grabbed my jacket."

It was a struggle to make out her friend's features with only the moonlight trickling through the foliage. "What I tell you about using my government. You bout crazier than a bag of raccoons, sitting out here in the dark. Wassup with you?"

"Bag of raccoons? Only you—always using those country ass sayings. And I love your name…almost as much as I love the woods. When someone's chasing you, it's one of the safest places to be."

KD laughed. "You always say that. Anyways, what's going on with you?"

"I don't know where to start."

"Well, it must be something major, or you wouldn't be here. So, spill it—wassup?"

JoJo looked straight ahead.

"You constipated? Just say it. I won't judge you. Let it out."

"Dax is in jail."

"For what?"

"I still don't have the official story. He still hasn't called."

"How long has it been?"

"Thursday will be three weeks?"

"Three?" She sighed deeply. "I'm sorry you're going through this, sweetie. Is there anything I can do?"

"I'll let you know, but that's not even what brought me here to see you. Remember Dax's cousin, Tank? I told you about how stupid he was, and how he treats the girls who live with him?"

"Yeah. Why? He got locked up too? Come to find out, I know the fool."

"No."

"What he do to you?"

"Nothing. Something was done to him."

"Don't tell me somebody blasted that ass? I wouldn't be one bit surprised. His reputation isn't the best."

"Nah. It wasn't anything like that. I blinked my eyes, and it was done."

"What was? You're confusing me. Stop talking in codes."

"He's dead."

"How? When?"

"Earlier today. It happened so fast."

"I'm confused."

"He was beating one... next thing I knew, she cold clocked him upside the head with a cast iron skillet. He never got up off the floor."

"Damn—hell of a way to go. What did y'all do? Is he still in the house?"

"We buried him."

"Are you being for real?"

"Real as a heart attack."

"You literally dug a ditch and put him in it. That's some wild shit." KD stared into the distance, digesting the news. "You got balls the size of King Kong's."

"Not really."

"You worried about the police?"

For the first time, JoJo realized her lack of concern. She paused before answering. "No."

"Like I said—you're tough as nails. Well golly, my little bit of gossip is nothing compared to what you shared."

"Noooo, don't say that. Please, tell me what's going on."

"Don't change the subject. My gawd—what are you going to do? Your life is such a fucking movie. Are you gonna stay in the house?"

"First, slow down. One question at a time. You're shooting them at me rapid fire. My brain is struggling to keep up. What am I gonna do? I don't know. I talked the dumb broads out of killing each other, dug a grave, washed my hands, ordered delivery, ate, and then ran over here. I haven't showered since this morning."

"P-U, and thanks for the visual."

"Whatever. My sweat smells better than roses. Let's get serious for a minute. I'm going to leave the area. I don't know when, but I see it coming. I promise I'll try to give you a heads up. But if I can't, just know–I'll find you again."

"We didn't cross paths for nothing. Everything happens for a reason."

"So true. I love you. You're the best friend I've ever had."

"Likewise."

"And now, you can never get rid of me. I'm H.I.V."

KD tilted her head to the side. "Oh—No! That has to be the worst analogy I've ever heard."

"I get what you're saying. Bad example. My point is—we're family. Maybe not by blood, but then again, maybe our great, great, grandfather's fathers were brothers.

"Yeah—and sold off the plantation together.

"Exactly. Now you're talking. You better get back in there, before Ethan comes out here looking for you. I can't stand that man."

"Nobody's worried bout his ass. He has his own disciplinary infractions. Ole boy is suspended. No explanation was provided."

"Suspended. *Ooooh*! De-Tails, please. I can't believe you held onto this juicy morsel the whole time we've been out here."

"Ms. G's son took a turn for the worse."

"I didn't know."

"Yeah—well, she took a leave of absence. She wasn't here the last couple of months. Things have been unruly since you left. Someone called Child Protective Services. I'm not sure who or why they did it, but I have my suspicions. Day before yesterday, a gang of people in church clothes interrogated us."

"What types of questions did they ask?"

"Real random shit. How are you treated? Do you go to school? How often do you attend therapy? Do I feel safe?"

"Which staff did they interview?"

"Who do you think?—Ethan Franks."

"Interesting. Was I mentioned?"

"Not during my meeting, but I haven't swapped notes with the others. I talked to Jeremy, but his ass was fried. He told them, 'I plead the fifth'."

"No he didn't!"

"Sure did."

"I miss my Matlock buddy. Please, tell him I said hello."

"Girl—you and them damn TV shows. I got you." KD rose and stretched. "I'd love to stay longer but it's time for me to creep back in here before your prediction comes true."

"I know the deal."

"It was good seeing you."

"Likewise. I forgot to mention—if you know anyone in need, I have weed."

"How much?"

"I didn't weigh it, but I'd guess a QP."

"Hook me up with an ounce."

"Sounds good. I could use the money. I have nothing."

"We'll talk more tomorrow. I'll be home by seven. Meet me at Hillside Park at a quarter after."

"I'm there."

"Are you out here by yourself?"

JoJo jumped from her seat. "I'm fine. I don't stay far. I've been putting these running shoes to work."

"Okay. Well—be safe, crazy girl."

The friends hugged. "I will. You too."

The moment felt like old times, and they'd just finished blazing.

I wish I could follow KD into the house, and climb into that hard twin bed. I wouldn't pay Ramona's snoring no mind.

Without a job or realistic action plan, she chickened out on bringing up them moving in together.

Hatima's taking me in a different direction.

18

PRESSURE MAKES DIAMONDS

*O*n Monday of the following week, Tina Yarbrough tearfully announced she was pregnant. By Wednesday, Ethan Franks' ten year career in Child Services, ended. The subsequent investigation uncovered his extortion of residents. He agreed to resign and repay the money embezzled. In the interim, his employer cut *"settlement"* checks for the *"aggrieved parties."* A few days later, KD called to say Mrs. G needed to see her. During the meeting, JoJo learned she made the list.

The five thousand dollars from *Stepping Stones* was just that. A few days before, she'd wondered how they'd eat. The change in fortune was an encouraging omen. She deposited three thousand in a savings account, and earmarked two for starting over.

Fuck Merle, and her coins!

Time nor distance lessened her resentment.

She's dead to me.

For a split second, she considered looking for her father, but decided, *sometimes, you have to leave well enough alone.*

Roxi's aunt in *B'more* offered to sublease her section 8. It was in a sketchy area, but it had three bedrooms with doors, two bathrooms, and wasn't far from the City center.

To JoJo, the details didn't matter. A roof over their heads, and forty-five minutes north of PG, sounded sweet. The carcass in the yard, imbued each with a heightened sense of urgency.

"I'll tidy the living and dining rooms. Roxi, you do the kitchen. Chanel…"

"I'll take care of the upstairs." She filled in the blank.

In three hours' time, they sanitized the house from top to bottom. Without the muddle and grime, they pictured it an inviting space, at one time.

Chanel plopped down on the couch. JoJo sat next to her. "Well got damn! I ain't never seen it look this good."

"Me either." Roxi agreed, from the kitchen doorway.

"I was bagging his shit when it dawned on me—It's gonna look like we all picked up and left?"

"Would that be strange?" JoJo asked.

"He told me his mother died, and his father was in prison. His grandma owned the place outright. I doubt anyone's checking for him. None of his people have ever come around."

She wondered if his neighbors would question his disappearance. After some deliberation, they agreed—"*jail*" was plausible.

Chanel pulled four one-hundred dollar bills from her bra. "In the process of going through his bureau, I found this." She'd planned to not mention it, but their flushed faces compelled her to keep it real.

"Nice—that's going to come in handy." JoJo smiled, floored by the honesty.

In less than an hour, JoJo filled six plastic tubs with her and Dax's wardrobes, the weed, comforters, a color TV, and miscellaneous cosmetics.

Conversely, the girls owned a ridiculous amount of stuff. "Would you consider giving some to the Salvation Army or throwing anything away?" One laughed like she'd heard a hilarious joke. The other looked at her like she'd sprouted a second head.

Tears flowed from Roxi's eyes as they stood in the living room for the last time. JoJo grabbed her hand. "What's wrong now?"

"I wish we could set this bitch on fire. I look around, and all I see, is all the places I got my ass whipped. Never again."

Chanel clapped. "I'm with you. F this hell hole! Let's get up out of here." She then turned to JoJo. "What do you say? We can't do it without you."

"I'm all in."

They didn't know, she had zero options. *We need each other!*

JoJo sat by the window, Chanel dourly sat in the middle, and Roxi concentrated on the road.

"How is it that Roxi has her license and you don't?"

As she applied a new coat of lipstick, Chanel replied, "Shucks—I'm glad. I'd rather ride."

"Shelly taught me how to be a getaway driver when I was ten."

"What?"

"No bullshit?" Roxi always said outlandish things, but this time JoJo actually believed her.

"Real talk. When I turned sixteen Tank took me to Motor Vehicles and I got my permit. I drove around like that for six months, then took the test twice before I finally passed it. Parallel parking is the hardest part for most, but that's where my lessons began."

"Wow!"

"She ain't lyin."

"You're good. I got this. Please buckle up! It's the law."

All three were hyped to leave DC. Chanel never liked it. No place paralleled Harlem. It was unfair to compare. Roxi wanted to be around family again. She hadn't seen her cousins in years, and prayed her mother's misdeeds, wouldn't be held against her. They'd assured her everything was cool, but she'd *"protect her neck,"* like her mother taught her.

JoJo wasn't heartless nor was she a killer. She didn't think burying a man in the yard was normal, but she was already in over her head.

No point in dwelling on a past that can't be changed.

She hadn't known Roxi and Chanel long, but felt their lives

were intertwined. Their shared secret could ruin all of their lives.

Got to keep them in sight!

Worry and doubt were pushed into the back of her mind and the hunger to survive kicked in. She'd yearned to be a real adult, and the stars conspired to make it happen.

I'm blessed! I have a sound mind. The money will sustain me for a few months. I can do this! I'm ready.

Interstate 295 led them directly into the city. From there, Roxi knew where she was going. She took Pratt Street, which passed *Harborplace* and the *Baltimore Aquarium*. It was early, but joggers and tourist were out and about and employees were entering the brightly painted buildings.

After cruising through a swath of public housing, followed by rows of form stone and red brick three-story federal style homes, they circled a massive park, before reaching their destination.

19

OPEN HOUSE

BALTIMORE, MD

*T*heir new home was at the end of the block across from an awning-making shop. A flat top blocked traffic while workers tied a large metal frame to the bed. While waiting, they surveyed their new domain.

The 2400 block of McElderry Street, comprised parallel rows of facing, two and three-story brick facades. The late-model cars, potted plants, Tonka toys, and painted screens were deceiving. They were moving into the middle of one of East Baltimore's largest open-air drug markets.

When the coast cleared, Roxi parked in front of the door. The trio climbed out the box truck. JoJo flexed, and stretched her arms and legs. "Looks pretty good from here."

Chanel got out, and sniffed. "Not what I expected. Even the air smell different."

Roxi leaned across the seat. "Listen to both of you. It's gonna be cool. Just wait, and see."

"Where are all those people going?" asked Chanel, astounded by the large crowd turning the corner. "They look shifty as hell."

Roxi thought, *she always finds a reason to fuss.* "Maybe they're tryna catch a bus."

"Yeah, right." Chanel shook her head. "Moving and eviction days give people a chance to see what folk have worth stealing. I wish we could've done this during the middle of the night."

JoJo wanted to kick off her shoes, and wiggle her toes. "True, but we're here now. Roxi, back up to the front door. We'll go in, and crack the windows."

Though it was small, there was ample room for them to coexist. The appliances and interior were in operational but due for upgrades. She and Roxi started bringing in bags while Chanel smudged the rooms with sage, and dotted each with sticks of incense. Pine-Sol eliminated some of the staleness, but a pervasive stench lingered.

When they broke for lunch, they took a walk to explore their *"new hood."*

The Monument Street corridor was the epicenter of their new universe. A liquor store, fried chicken or chop suey joint, sat on every corner. Five and dimes, shoe stores, clothing boutiques, and pawn shops served a steady stream of customers. A large, municipal market sold fish, meat, and fresh vegetables. They were blown away by the variety of sweet, and savory options, but a few people cautioned—*"Get it while you can! After six, that shit's dead. "*

After unloading everything, they returned the rental to a nearby depot. Unable to get a cab to stop, they asked a passerby for assistance. *"Everyone in Baltimore gets around in hacks."* The men beeping and yelling at them throughout the day now made sense.

A retired longshoreman dropped them off. He picked up riders, *"mainly nurses from Hopkins,"* to support his gambling habit. *"My lady thinks I have a girlfriend, as much I spend, at the track. I keep telling her—after 50 years and three children, I ain't studying no ova women."*

JoJo took his number and promised to use his service again.

Mrs. Richardson, their neighbor to the right and Biz, a childhood friend of Roxi's, who lived across the street, were sitting on their respective front steps. The girls rested on theirs. Roxi spoke, but the woman jeered, plucked her cigarette butt on the sidewalk and withdrew without speaking.

In response to the brushoff, she hollered, *"Fuck her!"* loud enough for everyone to hear it.

Mr. Rucks, the white-haired owner of the deli across the street, came to the door, and waved. Though legally a resident of Rosedale, he'd owned the property for years, and regarded the community, as his own. They thought it was odd his store wasn't partitioned with bullet proof glass, until she saw the pump under the counter. His *"zero tolerance for riff raff"* policy, kept their end of the block calm. He was soft-spoken, but took no shit, and the hoppers respected his *gangster*. The proud Korean War vet, was a godsend. Having him nearby, made them feel safer.

Biz came over, and started sweet-talking Chanel.

"What's that about? He acted real familiar." JoJo noted.

"Sure did—but Chanel likes confidence."

"Let's see where this goes."

Hours later, the threesome set out for *"Fells Point"*, located a mile away. They wanted to check out the waterfront, and *Super Linens* on S. Broadway, a Main Street the shopkeeper suggested they visit.

What awaited them was nothing like they'd pictured. Instead of a clearly delineated area for shopping—shoe outlets, bakeries, dress and smoke shops, scratch and dent liquidators, apartments, dive bars and churches, lined several interconnecting blocks. It was a lot to take in.

It wasn't long before they reached their destination. Inhabiting a prime corner location, the discount store's huge sign was hard to miss. Also, the *old man* had pumped it up like it was a sight to behold.

The place was a disorganized mess, and smelled of moth balls, but the prices were hard to resist. After spending more time than they'd intended sifting through racks of towels, wash cloths, curtains, rugs, and sheets, they purchased several apiece. Each also picked out items to personalize her room.

Of the many restaurants they passed, one excited Chanel.

She made them promise they'd visit before returning home. Although each was tired, a sit down dinner would hit the spot. They'd see the docks and boats, another time.

They entered the small eatery, and found it empty. Chanel tucked three menus under her arm, and pointed to a table along the far wall. Seconds later, a big-boned, fifty-something year old with a toothy smile, plodded forward, wiping her hands on her apron. "Hola! *(Hello!)* Perdón por tu espera *(Sorry for your wait)*."

With a fluency that shocked Roxi and JoJo, Chanel responded. "No No No – Gracious. Como esta ud? *(How are you?)*"

"Muy bien." *(Very good)*

"Tienes un buen restaurant. *(You have a nice restaurant)* We're happy you're open. It smells so good in here. Lo siento *(I'm sorry)* – Lo Chanelica, esto es *(I'm Chanelica, and this is…)* JoJo, and Roxi."

Both looked at her in awe.

"Everyone has called me Mama Si, for as long as I remember. It's nice to meet you all, and it's so great you've come."

"Now that I've talked to you." Chanel stood up, and inched closer to her. "I want some of what you're cooking for yourself?"

The woman laughed, and dabbed her glistening eyes.

Chanel collected the menus, and pushed them aside. "I know you've got something special in the pot."

"*Ah* – you remind me so much of my Ana. Stay put. Luis will bring out some empanadas, and Coca Ricos."

"Nice—muchas gracias!" *(Thank you very much!)*

When they were alone again, JoJo asked, "So…when did you find time to learn Spanish?"

Looking cheerier than either had ever seen her, she replied, "Spanish is my first language."

"I didn't know. That's kinda cool."

"The owner and I, are Puerto Ricans. I came to the mainland when I was eight to live with an uncle who died when I was thirteen. I've been on my own ever since. It's been a while since I've had anyone to speak it with. I'm a little rusty, but Mama

Si was polite enough not to mention it. When I saw the menu, I knew this place would be da bomb. She's doing everything herself. It's a genuine one woman show. I love it!"

"Chanelica?" asked Roxi with a grin, before looking into the distance.

Chanel hooted, and banged on the table. "Yeah, yeah yeah. She's an old timer, and Chanel wasn't going to cut it. I gave her something she could feel. It's from my baptismal. Shhhhh."

The matron returned five minutes later, and placed several large platters and bowls, in front of them. "Aqui esta! (*Here it is!*)"

"Ohhh, Maaaa-ma Siiiii," intoned Chanel. "Fried maduros (*plaintains*), yucca, potato salad, Arroz con Pollo (*chicken with yellow rice*). Is that cerdo (*pork stew*)? *Ohhh*. This mofongo smells amazing? Flan too? Ladies, we're dining like royalty."

Luis shuffled behind with plates, silverware, napkins, and the promised empanadas, and sodas.

"Enjoy, senoritas."

"Gracious, Mama Si."

Roxi grabbed a bowl. "I'm starved."

Chanel fanned the fragrant steam rising towards her face. "Me too!" She lowered her voice. "Doesn't she remind y'all of a grandma?"

Roxi looked around. "I sure miss mine. All right, big sis. I'm trusting you. This better be good."

"Better than sex."

JoJo said few words during the meal. The spread looked and smelled fine, but Chanel's comment had her ready to go. She wished she felt the same, or possessed similar recollections. Merle didn't remind her of anything fond, and she certainly never cooked, or shared recipes.

She ate a few plantains, and picked over some paella, before throwing in the towel. In contrast, her associates smacked, and gnawed like feral hogs. She wasn't alone, but it was the loneliest she'd felt in a long while.

20

BIZ

*T*he girl's first week culminated with the *Soldiers' Day Block Party*, a celebration for friends and relatives, lost to violence. OGs and New Jacks showcased their toys, played the dozens, and swigged brown liquor, while *"Dance"* and *"Best Dressed"* contests, mesmerized the elders and children. A cookout, held in a pocket park, was a celebrated Eastside, July ritual. Dope boys donated meat for the grill, shared stories about loved ones, and let off albino pigeons, in their memory.

A reunion was planned for that night. Gus, the first guy to welcome them to the neighborhood, gave them passes. Roxi and Chanel were ecstatic. Wrapped up in the delight of the invite, JoJo panicked when her own attire, came into focus.

The dress she wore to the *Crossroads*, sat on her bed. She'd already put her other *nice* outfit away—a mesh, pink and aqua green, short set.

Neither were her style, but her baby told her they were nice, and she'd taken him at his word. While both were beautiful, she didn't have the confidence required to pull them off. Over the years, a desire to defy convention, and irk Merle led to many laughable choices. Fashion and styling, still weren't strong suits.

Her eyes landed on the designer garments hanging in the closet. She had an epiphany—*Why not go with what works!*

Dressed in a teal polo, dark wash Girbaud's, and a ball cap, JoJo felt more womanly than ever. Thicker in the chest and waist,

Dax's clothes clung to her curves. His Js (*Air Jordan 8 "Aqua"*) were too big, but she wrapped thick wads of toilet paper around her heels, until they fit like gloves.

Roxi cornrowed her mop in a unique pattern, but a major change was on the horizon. She didn't know the direction she wanted to go, but a perm was out of the question. Her one salon experience had been a nightmare. She touched her ear, recalling the sting. The sound of sizzling pomade was forever etched in her brain. She slumped in the chair and cried, but neither the stylist, nor Merle, showed concern. While turning off the bathroom light she thought, *never again!*

Roxi saw her first. "JoJo, you look great, but you know what people will think."

She smiled sweetly. "What?"

"That you play for the other team?

"Ha! Whatever that means. Besides, once they get a look at you, they'll forget I'm there."

Roxi raised her arms, and spun around like a ballerina. Cream-colored lace shorts, and a matching halter, accentuated her slender form. It looked comfy, but left little to the imagination. A colorful dragon tattoo snaked from her shoulder to her lower back. Nude t-strap heels, blond bob wig, frosted pink lipstick, and a suede cross-body fringe, finished her sexy look.

Chanel, never to be outshined, wore a black cat suit with patent leather stilettos. Her body was bananas, so she kept her accessories simple—large hoops, a clean face, and her hair, finger waved. It was humid as hell, and she planned to dance, and didn't want to end up looking like the Joker.

JoJo had seen them dolled up before, but they now somehow appeared–*cleaner.* "Y'all are going to get us in trouble."

The festive atmosphere persisted, after the earlier revelries. Their path to the venue was dotted with celebrations. As far as their eyes could see, double-parked cars lined the right side of the two-way street. As they approached, the whistling and catcalling began:

"Here, kitty, kitty. Can I get your number?"

"Is that a camel toe?"

"Man—she got a fat burger."

"Lor miss vanilla wafer. What's your name?"

"Damn, shorty. Did that tat hurt?"

"Will you marry me? Or at least, carry my first born."

"Hell no! Leave us alone," barked Chanel.

"Eat a dick then, you big-headed bitch!"

It was as if they'd never seen nice-looking women, or each had just gotten out of jail.

"Baltimore niggas are plain nasty."

"Who responds to that shit?"

"Girl—I don't know."

One guy grabbed Roxi's arm, forcing JoJo to intervene. She stood her ground. He backed off. Dudes clowned him for causing a scene. The girls loved JoJo's demeanor. Her shielding gestures deterred others with similar designs, and made them feel protected.

Sexiness in all forms lined Milton Ave. From the whips with dipped rims, and diamonds crusted medallions on display, they knew, these were the Big Boys. Some, posted up with blunts of gas, and red cups, runneth over. Others, entertained with garish theatrics, as rap blasted from their subwoofers.

They soon passed another group of guys, and the harassment resumed. Not wanting to appear irritated, pressed or thirsty, they smiled and waved, but didn't pause for conversation.

Chicks were styling and profiling too. Instead of readying for a good time, a few looked distressed. One group, watched the trio like hawks. The sextet known as the *Ball Fiddy Clique*, sized them up like rival fighters. In the end, each side weighed and measured, the quote unquote competition, and found the other wanting.

The *American Legion* was abuzz with light-hearted energy. People laughed and hugged in every direction. People raised their chins, and cleared a path as the girls inched deeper into the interior. After a while, Biz's distinct snicker stood out.

JoJo crept up behind him, and tapped his shoulder. "I like your technique."

"What do you mean?"

"You're standing by the watering hole."

"Ha! I see you down with that Mutual of Omaha's Wild Kingdom shit too."

"Hell yeah. Sometimes, it's the only thing worth watching."

"Word. You can learn a lot from animals and nature. You drinking?"

"Thanks for noticing us standing here too."

"Go head with dat, Rochelle. Come show me some love." He pulled her into his embrace.

"Don't be putting my b.i. out there like that. Put that Rochelle shit in the crypt. You hear me?"

"I hear you, foxy Roxi. Remember—I know you from way back. Now that we're cool again, what y'all drinking?"

"I haven't made up my mind. How y'all feelin'—light or dark?"

"Fuck it. Let's get right?" Chanel answered for the crew. "Dark, it is. Biz—Henny times three."

Roxi could drink them all under a table, but she added, "I'ma do my best to stay on both feet."

"Oh shit! Y'all love hen-dog too? Man! I love chicks that can hang. I'll be right back."

The crowd had quadrupled since they'd entered. As Biz struggled for a spot along the bar, they were happy he'd waded into the mayhem for them.

"Where you from?" asked the guy next to Roxi, staring at his G-Shock.

She gave him the once over and found him pleasing. Tall, copper-colored skin, with golds on both sides of his front teeth, a small mustache and short hair. *He's a little lean, but his foot print and fingers …Mmmh, long suck-able dick*—a must for anyone she banged for fun.

"Murlend."

"Really? You got a real seductive accent. Like you from down South."

"What are you tryna say? Do I sound country to you?"

"Nah, boo. Come awn. Where you from?"

"Ever heard of Potomac?

"Can't say I have. Is that near the Eastern Shore?"

"You're cute. It's close to DC."

"How long will you be here? Are you visiting family or something?"

"Nah, I live here."

"Where?"

"Not far."

"Well, take my number. I like your smile. What are you doing later?"

"Not sure yet." She pointed to her companions. "We—me and my peoples, haven't discussed it."

"Well, I'd love to take you to get something to eat."

"Sounds fun." She handed him a pen and a piece of paper. "What's your name?"

"Keefy."

"I'm Roxi."

He scribbled something then handed her the pen and paper back. "I won't take up too much more of your time. Looks like main man is back with y'all drinks. Call me."

"Sure does." He was gone when she turned back around. Though he exited abruptly, she found it sexy. He wrote his phone number, and *"It's big"* on the paper. She marveled at how he'd known.

Biz distributed red cups. JoJo sniffed the concoction. "What's this? It's not Hennessey."

"Try it before you knock it! It's called Incredible Hulk."

Roxi took a sip. "Ohhhh! It's strong as hell, but tastes pretty good."

Chanel smiled. "Yummy. But my question is–what makes it green?"

"Hypnotic. Some new shit!"

Biz finished his, and was itching to cut a rug. "Y'all smelling all sweet. Come on—I see you wiggling that ass. Let's dance."

"You're nasty."

"Shiid! I'ma man."

Chanel put her empty cup on a ledge, and grabbed his hand. "I'm down."

"Cool." Roxi finished chewing a mouthful of ice and took hold of his other. JoJo declined. "I'll people-watch instead."

Three songs later, Roxi and Chanel's alter egos made their first appearances. As Roxi backed her ass up on Biz, Chanel pushed him to the side. She licked her lips while rubbing and grinding the younger girl's hips. JoJo found it odd because any other time, she treated her with contempt. Neither were *"into women,"* but knew the spectacle caused a stir.

People talking about the *"shorties on the floor wildin'!"* made her scan the hall until she spotted them. *Sure nuff!* It was *her* girls.

Gus walked towards them, so she headed there too.

As if he felt her stare, he turned and their eyes connected. He waved her over. *"Ehhh!* You made it. That's what up. Give me some love."

She gave him the hug, but felt uncomfortable.

"Your home girls out there showing off."

She laughed. "Yeah. I can't take them nowhere."

"Nah—they're getting their life. Let's join them."

"I'll go with you, but I don't dance."

"Come on." He grabbed her hand and pulled her along.

When they reached the dance floor, the energy was electric. Roxi and Chanel had two poor souls, backed up against the wall, rock hard, ready, and sweating. JoJo and Gus were tickled. He told her, "One of those succors is my ace."

JoJo was unfamiliar with most of the music mixed that evening. It was too homegrown. She couldn't get into it. As the DJ blended two hits, a stampede joined the merriment. Light on his feet, Gus two-stepped with the beat. He grabbed her finger and teased, "Come on. You know you wanna do it. Please."

She pulled away, but leaned in closer so he could hear her over the 808s. "Oh, no. I'm good. Matter fact, I'm going to get out of the way."

"Aww—you holding out on me."

"I told you, I don't dan…" JoJo paused as the sea of people parted at her feet.

"Scuze me," shouted the petite, dark-complected girl, pushing her aside.

"You're excused. Gus—you better get your bird."

Tashia spun in her direction. "Or what? Don't talk to him. Talk to me."

"Or we can handle this…" JoJo only got out a few words before he intervened.

"Pause. Both of y'all. Tasia—why are you running up on me like the law? I'm bout sick of your shit. You don't even know this girl yet you selling wolf tickets. Ain't shit going on. It's a damn party. Go have fun. While you're at it, find you a lil boyfriend. Stay out of my business."

Undeterred by her stature, Tasia looked at JoJo, and smirked. "Clearly, she ain't from round here. I can back up anything, I say. You best tell your little friend about me." With her right hand on her hip, she waved her left index finger. "I'll let you get back to whatever it is you're doing, but I'm watching you."

"I'm a grown ass man. Don't watch me. Watch our daughter."

Before trudging away, she fired back. "Fuck you, Gus. You'll get yours one day."

He gripped his nuts. "Bitch—you wish!"

After laughing off the clash, he turned to JoJo. "So, what about that dance?"

"I'll pass."

21

C.R.E.A.M.

*J*oJo had never been an early riser, but now, seven a.m. was her favorite hour. Everyone else, if home, was fast asleep.

Her pre-game ritual always started with brewing a pot of coffee. A large cup with Hazelnut creamer, shook off the lingering vestiges of sleep. White toast with jelly, and a bowl of Frosted Flakes or Farina with butter and brown sugar, were typical eats.

While breaking her fast, she read the newspaper, a few chapters of a book, or wrote in her journal. Local politics was unexciting and monotonous, but she found Global affairs, enlightening. Jerry Springer and Maury went off at eleven, and rounded out her routine. The fights and paternity test results were comic relief, and made her appreciate being drama free.

The phone and electric were on, once she put both in her name. Chanel had no ID, and Roxi's mother wrecked her credit when she was a baby. Unlike the girls, she wasn't into living without furniture. The couches, TV stand, étagère, and kitchen table, purchased from Value City at *Eastpoint Mall*, weren't much, but made the space more inviting.

Roxi's family turned out to be a trip. The only thing they wanted from her, was to *"hold a few dollars,"* and talk shit. Thankfully, her aunt seemed official. She came through in every way promised. Even if the roommates thought they paid too much, JoJo saw the bigger picture. Their chances of finding something newer, and cheaper, were slim and none.

Her small room had two south facing windows. The full-sized bed, set her back two-hundred dollars, but being off the floor was priceless. She was camping by the standard she was raised, but it didn't matter. Every day she woke up feeling good about herself, and did whatever she wanted. After close to two years of surviving on her wits, she'd go hungry before tucking tail, and begging for pity. *The Pierre's can keep their dough!*

From the outset, a house of women was an ambitious goal, but JoJo, Roxi, and Chanel peacefully coexisted. She'd never question their motivations. It wasn't her place. After all, she'd never wanted for basic necessities. *I can't imagine the problems they've faced.*

Both of them, despite diverging outlooks and choices, were battle tested. She wasn't, and knew they could teach her many lessons.

If the circumstances were different, I could be with them.

When things quieted down, house rules were set in stone. Numero Uno, Safety in numbers—*"No going out alone,"* and number two,—*"No freakin off with each other's dates."*

Plenty of guys from the neighborhood tried to holla, but *"around the way tricks,"* were off limits. Hurt feelings, affected the bottom line. Home remaining *"Zen"*, made sense.

It took a while to adjust to the rhythm and sounds of the Eastside. Outside of the few times she traveled to the library on N. Broadway, she didn't venture far from the house.

The moniker, *'Bodymore, Murdaland'*, wasn't an exaggeration. Ninety-three was the city's bloodiest summer on record. She often wondered if they were part of a government experiment—*"The effects of living in a combat zone."* At night, gun shots and sirens, were common as birds whistling at dawn. The non-stop traffic heading in and out of *Johns Hopkins*, reminded her of the constant danger. DC's homicide rate was notorious, but it's impact felt foreign.

Their block stayed hot, night and day. JoJo had never seen

so many personalities packed into one place. Three generations living together was common. People made up their own rules, and governed themselves accordingly. Arriving home to a stranger lounging on your steps was par for the course. A car wash, candy stand or dress shop, were apt to pop up on any day of the week. Complain about the inconvenience, and you may get cursed out, or entangled in real beef.

On the whole, JoJo's days were mundane. She normally showered and dressed by noon. Then, she listened to their chat line messages and mapped out the day. This was their primary method of setting up *"dates."*

During their first month, boredom, take out, and taxis, ate up a chunk of her payout. The cash Chanel unearthed, was never discussed again. She stocked the cabinets once, then it fell on JoJo to ensure they ate. The girls wondered where she was getting money, but hunger kept them humble.

After weeks of public transportation, JoJo understood its limitations. Buses were irregular, jam-packed, and slow, with spotty AC. Cabs were unreliable too. You call, they honk, and if you don't come out running, they gun it. The subway was as useful as an amusement park trolley. Owings Mills to Charles Center Station, were the limits of the run. If traveling from the East to the Westside of town—*hmmmph, you're shit out of luck!*

If they asked in advance, the hacker, Mr. Kenny, drove them to their destination, and waited. JoJo had already joined him for a few races. The ride to Laurel, and the view from the bleachers was cool. The horses smelled, but it beat sitting in the house, wishing conditions were different.

Dax was on her mind all the time. The pangs of desire wouldn't die. Her body hungered for his touch. Every day, she clutched his clothes to her chest, and imagined him flexing in the mirror. She buried the shoe box of letters she wrote him, in the top of her closet, until she figured out what to do with them. Throwing them away felt irreverent.

Her eighteenth birthday came, and went without celebration.

The girls didn't know, and she doubted, they'd cared. She missed KD, and wondered how she was getting along. A listening friend was a blessing she mourned when it was gone.

Once she found her rhythm, she planned to reach out, and treat her to a night on the town. Of all the people left behind, *their* separation, impacted her most.

Gus moved the remaining three ounces of weed by bagging up six hundred dollars' in dimes, opposed to the seventy-five each, she originally needed. *"The B'More flip is different."* His eagerness to go hard, compelled her to give him a second look. *"I like helping you out. You can even keep my cut."* Though he wasn't an intellectual, she figured, *I could use him for something.*

They needed a car, but it wasn't going to happen unless JoJo took the initiative. Biz referred her to a guy with a dealers' license. She wanted a Honda or Toyota. He supposedly had several of both.

Roxi staggered into the kitchen, grabbed a bowl, then the milk jug, out the fridge. Her sluggish movements, spoke of a rough night. JoJo was happy to see her up.

"I need you to go with me, later today. And throw on those jeans shorts."

"Sure thing!" said Roxi, sponging a dribble escaping her lip.

The girls walked up Orleans to *Old Town Mall*, less than a mile away. Chanel didn't feel well, so she stayed in bed.

A throwback to a bygone era, many of the outdoor shopping center's stores were shuttered. Sprinkled between Asian hold outs, were spirited stalwarts, waiting for metamorphosis or death.

Located at the far end of the quad, *Legends Barber Shop*, remained steadfast during the city's most tumultuous years. Historic concert posters, citations bestowed on the establishment, and photos of African-American greats, covered the walls. Open since the sixties, the owner still serviced regulars on Tuesdays, and dignitaries, by appointment.

Country, the auto salesman, cut hair in the last chair. They passed at least twenty guys before hearing his baritone voice. He was ready to deliver the punch line, when he spotted them, and winked. "And guess what!" he told the patrons, hanging onto his every word. "The mofo didn't even sign the lease."

"Are you serious?" an older gentleman shouted.

"I ain't owe him a dime."

Spectators burst into applause.

"You's a lucky mutha."

"Watch your language," admonished a lady with babies.

The humbled elder, accepted the rebuke. "I wasn't going to say it."

Country removed his smock, and tossed it on his station. "Excuse me fellas, but I have a prior engagement."

"Eh! What about me?" shouted a guy who'd been on the phone.

"What about you? I said, be here at ten."

"Duty called. Come on. You know how it is."

"Yeah? Well—get breakfast and kick back."

"All right, but how long will you be?"

He walked over, and put his arms around the girls. "This nigga. Forgive my little cousin's manners." With eyes fixed on Roxi, he licked and chewed, his bottom lip. "How y'all doing?"

"We're good. I'm JoJo. This is my friend, Roxi. She's the one with a license."

"Oh, Aiight. I spoke to you on the phone. Biz's peoples. Cool, cool, cool. Y'all ready?"

"Ready for what? Are we going someplace? I assumed the cars were here?"

"Nah. I can't park them on the mall. The garage is around the corner. Don't be scurd. Y'all can ride with me."

"Okay."

"I'll catch you fine folk on the flip side. Timmy—don't get no crumbs in my chair."

With the girls trailing, the trio exited the building. He disarmed the alarm on a grey 745 with dark tint, parked at the bottom of the block. Guys from the projects, across the street, came over and showed love. He shooed them away. "Go ahead. It's unlocked."

JoJo opened the curbside door, and Roxi climbed in the rear. A Black Ice Little Trees, freshened the air. Rap blared from the speakers.

"I can't front—this is a sweet ride."

"You ain't lying, but don't get too comfortable. We may need to jump out."

Seconds later, he climbed in, and peeled off. He whipped around the corners like a Grand Pre racer, disregarding stop signs, and nearly hitting, a distracted pedestrian. At a red light, he adjusted the interior mirror to get a better look at his rear passenger.

He pulled into *Sammy's*, hit a remote button, and a roll-up door ascended. From the exterior, the garage appeared vacant, but inside, it teemed with activity. He pointed to a four-door hunter green Camry. "Go on…kick the tires. I'll be right over."

"All right."

The girls got out, and inspected the exterior. He returned with keys, opened the door and started the engine. It hummed. JoJo and Roxi tinkered with the bells and whistles, while he explained the vehicle's history.

"I bought it from a guy out Edgemere. He claimed it was his mom's. She'd recently passed, and he needed cash for the burial. No doubt about it, he was a crack head, but I didn't ask a bunch of questions. I've had it for a month. 79,000 miles, clean carpet and seats, sun roof, power everything. There's nothing at all wrong with it. I'd been thinking of saving this one for myself. What cha'll think?"

Roxi brushed the dash. "I love it."

JoJo was more apprehensive. "It's nice–for sure, but how

much you want for it? This doesn't look like a putt-putt to me."

He flashed a devilish grin. "I'm just showing you what's in stock, so you know your options."

Certain it wasn't in their price range, she wondered, *what's he up to?* "That's fine. We appreciate the information, but show me what eight hundred dollars will buy."

He pointed to the opposite side of the shop. "You can take the Mazda, or I guess, I could let the blue Taurus go."

"That's it?" She hadn't expected an Audi or a Cressida, but the selections were doo-doo. The white 626 had a grey driver's side door, and grass had sprouted under the Ford's back tires.

"Don't look so disappointed. Maybe we can come up with something else." He paced back and forth a few times, then stopped. "There's an auction coming up if you feel like waiting. I thought you were ready."

"I am ready. We're not seeing eye to eye."

"Check it—I want thirty-five hundred for the Camry, but I'll sell it to you at cost. Give me your eight-hundred today, and drive off. You can bring me something every week til we square."

They got out the car. He was a smooth talker, but JoJo did the math in her head. *Seventeen-hundred at two hundred dollars a week, for eight and a half weeks, or a little over two months.* "Hear me out. Not saying it isn't worth it, but that's steep for us. We don't have it like you."

He sucked his teeth, and acted like he was thinking. "Three Gs, and Miss Roxi will be my date for the evening. We can finalize the payment arrangement tomorrow."

JoJo thought she'd seen him checking her out, but wasn't certain. He'd done an outstanding job of concealing his perversion.

Roxi loved watching JoJo work her magic, but thought the prior twenty seconds were the funniest. Country was on the husky side, but easy on the eyes. She liked his build, bow legs, and sly smile. *I hope he's gentle and eats pussy.*

"I like how you cut to the chase. I'll give you a stack—today, and owe you fifteen hundred, which I'll pay off—two hundred a week."

"Done deal, but we kicking it all night." He winked at his pledge.

JoJo didn't need to look at Roxi. Older men were her forte. "Let's have that conversation early. Misunderstanding is poisonous."

"Shordy, you cocky as shit, but I fucks with you. She better be worth it. Go on, check out y'all new whip. I'll grab some temp tags. I'ma throw those in for free. You got thirty days to get to the MVA. Let me also find something for you to write your address down. Here are the keys."

She pulled on Roxi's sleeve. "Don't hurt him."

JoJo had seen Merle haggle enough to know, there should've been more back and forth, but they needed this ride. With Country, they drove off, without signing on a line.

If the barter bothered Roxi, she didn't show it. She blissfully flexed, and rapped while speeding up the road. For peace of mind, JoJo went with the flow. *If her skills are what she claims, I might not come out of pocket again. Wouldn't that be something!*

They turned the corner, and ran smack into a pack of broads, dancing in the street. As they passed, Tasia gave them the middle finger.

After parking, JoJo hopped out. Roxi stayed put. Curious about the hold up, she tapped on the glass. "Wassup?"

"Should we come back later?"

Initially, JoJo hadn't popped off out, of respect for Gus. Now—scrapping with her, simply didn't make sense. *Something has to give!* She wasn't sure how much longer she could refrain from reacting to her scare tactics and passive aggressive threats.

"No. Fuck them! We live here. If we leave because of them, we best prepare to be tormented every day. Fear is false evidence appearing real. We're bout to sit our pretty asses on our steps, and leave when we're good and ready. Not a minute sooner. Those cockroaches are beneath us. Those bitches don't matter."

"You're right."

"Better yet—let's go in. I'm tired. It's already been a long ass day."

"To hell with them! Besides, I need to call Country."

"Exactly."

The house was noiseless when they entered. The aroma of Chanel's spicy shrimp spaghetti, made their stomachs rumble. JoJo powered the TV, and laid across the couch. She wanted to calm her nerves before feeding her face. Roxi headed upstairs to take a shower.

Grateful for dinner, she knocked on Chanel's door to see how she was faring. "*Sweetest Taboo*" played in the background, but there wasn't a verbal response. Tired of waiting, she turned the knob. Through the crack, she saw her riding Biz, reverse cowgirl.

Aaaah shit! Get it, get it! No wonder this bitch can't hear me.

"You like that?"

"*Mmmmh,*" she moaned in response.

"Don't slow down." He smacked her ass. "Mmmmh, don't stop!"

Roxi hadn't thought about sex with Biz in years. *The dick was kinda big. Then, she remembered how easy he got whipped. I hope that zap out shit was a phase.* Neither lover noticed her back up, and out, the same way she'd entered.

22

IT'S OUR ANNIVERSARY!

"I appreciate, all you've done."

JoJo marked her page, and turned to Roxi. "What do you mean?"

"Getting us moved in. Making sure we have food in the fridge. Even, staying on me about cleaning. This is the best living situation I've ever had."

"I'm happy, you're happy. It's nothing."

"Maybe to you. I've been studying people since I was young. I've never met anyone like you. You have a gift. I see how you handle lames, and hold casual conversations with bosses. You make everybody feel important. Soon, nobody's going to be able to fuck with you."

JoJo wondered, *where's this headed?*

"I think you're a dope chick too. I really love what you do with my hair. Thus far—knowing you has been a pleasure."

"So you know I'm about my paper."

"When you put your mind to it."

"No doubt.

Unlike Chanel, who bagged trade daily, the younger one, worked in spurts. She'd been happier, and no longer complained of nightmares, but still wasn't carrying a full load.

JoJo constantly nagged about the voice messages she neglected to return. Making matters worse, Keefy kept her placated with fifths of liquor and purple.

"I'm digging your style mama. I've given our situation some thought and I want you to be my manager. You tell me what to do. I'm down for whatever."

"Rewind—I'm no pimp. We're a team. Do your part, and I'll do mine. When you say you're going to do something, do it. Never leave one of us hanging. Beyond that—take your shot."

"I can't speak for everyone, but I need help. I'm young and want to have fun, but I also like eating. You always make sure we're good. That's a job, if you ask me."

JoJo's eyes opened wide. "You think?"

Chanel entered with her face covered in Noxzema. "What the hell y'all talking about?"

JoJo and Roxi laughed. "I was telling Rox we don't need to define what we have. Everything will be fine. I'm loyal to both of you, and vice versa. I'll never steer either of you wrong. We all want a safe place to lay our heads."

She smiled. "That's more than anyone else has done for me. Shiiid, that's all I need."

"Ain't that the truth!" Roxi left the room.

"I wanna get money. The whole time we was fucking with Tank, I knew the nigga hustled backwards. He loved to nickel and dime tricks, like my ass was a bag of crack. We could've done less for more, if the muthafucker would've had sense enough to listen."

"Well—I'm not him. Tell me all your ideas."

Chanel sat down on the couch, and turned on the stereo. "Thank gawd! I gave him everything I had, but he also wanted my soul."

"So, how about we figure out a strategy, and really get this party started. Plus, we need to pay for that car out there."

"Without a doubt. Baltimore ain't ready for us. There's so much money to be had."

Roxi returned, carrying the strawberry shortcake she copped from Rose's Bakery.

"You would whip that out when my face is covered in this

shit. That cake looks amazing. Did you get it from Northeast Market?

"Yup! The stall by the back door."

"*Mmmm.* What's the occasion?"

"We're celebrating our anniversary."

"I'm down. What happened on this day in history?" Chanel asked.

JoJo swiped a dollop of frosting, and put the finger in her mouth. "Mmmmh, that's delicious."

Roxi pondered the question before answering. "We became family."

Having others to lean on, was all any of them ever dreamed of.

Roxi's pledge made JoJo feel, part of a team. She rubbed her hands together. "If that's the case, cut me a big piece." For the first time, her contribution felt meaningful.

An older lady Roxi met at the market gave them their first lead.

"*Pulaski Highway—it ain't for the faint of heart. Crossing the street is treacherous. White, Black, Latina—mainly resting travelers, and truckers. You've got your Romeos, and your crazies, but that's everywhere. When I was out there—I always made out. Get your money, honey, but be safe.*"

As they pulled into the Crown filling station, they were struck by how inhospitable the expanse appeared. Seedy, rent-by-the-hour motels, lined the concourse with a few topless bars and mini shopping centers, sprinkled in between. "What's your gut telling you?" asked Chanel.

"I'm not going to say no right away. Let's be open minded, and check out a few spots."

Their first stop, *The Stardust Lounge*, had the biggest and brightest marquee. Dark haired men in jogging suits occupied every chair. Most were immersed in private conversations, but their accents were Russian. A few looked up, but none appeared interested in Roxi and Chanel's offering. After a similar reception at two other bars, they agreed this wasn't their track. They hopped back in the car, and headed downtown a/k/a Plan B.

Their next destination was a quarter mile stretch of S. Baltimore Street known as *'The Block'*. Bumper to bumper traffic greeted them. Porn and toy shops, peep shows, and titty bars, lined both sides of the strip. All agreed, the scenery was more their speed.

It's nearness to City Hall, was a throwback to a bygone era; a time when hustlers, blue bloods, and politicians, openly shared anecdotes and beers. In truth, nothing had changed. The bankrupt, curious and unfulfilled, were out and about, ready to spill their bits. Men in suits, mixed with D-boys, clergymen, and starlets, without being noticed. Whores of different persuasions, offered company to those able to pay them.

They discovered a Greek, Thaddeus Samos, owned the *"real estate,"* a discreet way of saying he controlled the commerce. His underling, *Mr. Whitefolks*, was an olive complected, polyester suit wearing, grease ball with a pompadour. He strong-armed pimps and fake thugs, and hollered at every piece of ass, breathing (*lady boys* included).

Once he got wind of their accent and origins, he pressured them even more. He recognized the girls' novelty and grossing potential, and thus, he pushed hard to add them to his stable.

"We're free agents." JoJo loved the look on his face. Pissed by the snub, he labeled the ladies *"Shady!"*

The smell of the hotdogs grilling in *Crazy 8's* window, enticed thousands of buyers each day. Open twenty-four seven, every caste and class, frequented the part restaurant, part old-school arcade. The girls introduced themselves to the ragtag community of regulars, and started *"making friends."*

A White gal, with a voluptuous body, stood out in the crowd of monochromatic faces. She had a wow factor that made grown men giggle like babies. Impossible to disregard, she walked hard, held her crown high, and seduced with the sureness of a siren.

JoJo wanted to learn her methods, and possibly add diversity to their clique. An encyclopedia of information, the *snow bunny* knew the ends and outs of the game.

The longer she observed her moves, the more her certainty increased.

Roxi didn't like her from jump. Chanel gave everyone a shot.

"Trust me—there's a way for all of us to come out on top."

23

GUS WHAT

*T*here was a death metal concert going on in JoJo's head. It pained her to part her eyes, but laying up past eight a.m. felt strange.

Why-o-why is the sun, so bright? She looked to her left at Gus softly snoring, and thought, *what a night!* She raised her head, threw back the covers, then jumped up, and closed the blinds. Afterwards, she sat on the bed, being careful not to wake him.

Her mouth was dry as hell, and tasted like bitter herbs. She sniffed, then took a sip from the cup on the side table. *Water.*

She massaged her sore eyelids, but it didn't help.

This was the kind of hangover, only another drink would fix. She'd heard her grandfather call it—*"Biting the dog that bit him."* She took a swig of vodka from the bottle on the floor, and prayed it did the trick.

This was their third or fourth time going 'there.' After each unplanned encounter, she swore it'd be their last. She hadn't planned for *"card night"* to turn into headboard-banging sex, but she didn't regret it either. The release was satisfying, and greatly needed.

Wrestling ended with a handshake, which led to a hug. Hugging, was heightened with a few rubs. Then kissing—gentle at first, but soon, with wild abandon. He sucked her tongue, and licked her gums, before nibbling on her bottom lip. She didn't resist. In truth, the sensation was splendid. Next thing she knew, her pants were off, and she was pushing his face into her crotch.

He usually hit it and dipped, but this time he lingered. She wasn't mad, but didn't know what it meant.

Though he shared his homeboys' business more than he should, she was confident their romps would remain secret. She'd been in Baltimore eight months, and no one had piqued her interest. He wasn't a catch, but would do in the interim. Besides, with the way she dressed, she questioned what a man *hollerin' at her* was into. Gus knew it was just fashion.

The first time he saw her shaved head, he traced around her hairline with his thumbs. *"A one against the grain, huh? Damn shawd— few chicks could get away with it, but you make it look good?"*

More than sex, JoJo believed he valued her insight and opinion. Since accepting her counsel, his income doubled. She also knew, he got off on the fact that everyone assumed she was a *"stud."* As long as he kept his mouth shut, people could feel, how they wanted.

She wasn't in love, but trusted him enough to be vulnerable. He accepted her non-negotiable terms—*"Don't waste my time!"* and *"Keep that simple bitch away from my doorstep!"* Tashia and Gus' relationship status wasn't a concern. The *baby mama* was a thorn in *"his"* side. If she had an inkling they messed around, she'd spazz on them both. Neither wanted that. She prayed he covered his tracks.

The phone rang.

She picked up the receiver. "Hello."

"Hey, JoJo. Sorry to call so late, or rather, early. Man— I'm glad I reached you. I need a big favor. That bitch, Kitty, just flaked on me. I need dancers for tonight."

She didn't know with whom she was speaking, but played along. "What's going on?"

"We give an afterhours party at this biker club at Baltimore and Smallwood. It's usually a bunch of old timers, and our boys, but I guarantee y'all will clear a G."

"How much?"

"You heard me."

"How?"

"I'll just say this—I'ma hit you off for coming through. Whatever tips and side deals y'all mastermind, are all you. I just want everyone pleased, when they leave."

"Ro – is this you?"

"Yeah, nigga. Who you thought it was?"

She cleared her voice. "My bad, yo. I ain't know. Hell yeah, we down. What time, and where do you need us to be?"

Nella introduced the girls to Bam, aka the "Triple bar king of the Bay." Rohan was his big brother. She figured—*that's how he got the number.*

"Are you familiar with Bon Secours?"

"Nah."

"It's ova west. Nella Blanco know where we be. We get it poppin round midnight. Get there by eleven, if you can. I'd like to chop it up for a few."

"Aight, we'll be there. Thanks again." She hung up the phone.

"Where are you going to be?" Gus' voice was hoarse.

"You're awake. Mornin'. Oh— just a new money stream."

"I swear, you're one of the smartest females I know."

"Told you—I'm working while most of the world's still asleep."

"I see. Ambition is sexy." He then pulled the covers back to reveal a protruding erection. "Amongst other things... Come here, girl."

"*Mmmmh,* my pleasure."

24

NUNYA

Gus and JoJo remained entwined well past noon. Considering, she was the stickler for house rules, one being—"guests out by eight a.m.," his presence felt a smidge hypocritical.

If it wasn't for Roxi, the policy wouldn't have been required. Her habit of bringing home *randoms*, who didn't respect boundaries, called for a strong reaction. Finding a *"strange yo"* in the bathroom, wearing nothing but his boxers, isn't a greeting anyone desires.

Before he dashed down stairs, she stopped him. "Nah—we're taking this walk together." He beamed. "Ard. Ain't no shame in my game."

The girls sniggered as the blushing pair entered the kitchen. Roxi was tightening Chanel's weave, and Nella was polishing her nails.

The lovers had been discrete about their affair, but after last night, everyone knew the deal. They respected her position— *"Let their minds roam free. Who I sleep with is no one's business."* They laughed when people asked if she liked *"bitches."*

Both were amazed she'd held out so long, but the bigger shock was her choosing Gus. He was no upgrade but he made their friend smile, so they gave him the benefit of the doubt. Never in a million years would they have picked him for her type. Dax was laid-back, suave and easy on the eyes.

125

Word on the street—he sold drugs, but partied more than he made sales. His squad harassed everyone exiting the corner store on Jefferson and Patterson Park. He dressed nice—*gold Figaro link, new kicks every week, designer jeans and tees*, but none of that impressed them. If he wooed JoJo, he couldn't be the *slouch* they expected.

"Good Morning," said JoJo, when staring elicited no response.

Chanel pushed the pile of hair covering her to the side. "Morning, Sunshine. Left you some jitter juice in the pot. I bet it's still hot. Sorry Gus, didn't know you'd still be here."

"No problem, at all. Coffee makes me shit."

JoJo frowned. "Thanks for sharing, but gross."

"Guess what," said Roxi, looking sad. "Someone broke out one of the car's back windows. I think Tashia had something to do with it."

"What!" JoJo exclaimed, confused by the news.

Roxi turned to Gus. "That's your baby mama, what do you think?"

"Square biz—Ion know."

"Ion know?" She hated the *dumb* grin on his face. "He don't know y'all."

All of them wondered, *who else could it be?*

They stayed to themselves, and never courted attention. Outside of Biz and Mr. Rucks, they didn't say anything to their neighbors. Most of them were *unbothered*, which suited them fine, because they wished to live low key.

JoJo spoke up. "Riding round with cardboard in the window ain't happening. You need to fix this."

Gus sent a fiend to *Crazy Ray's* junk yard for a replacement. Two hours and sixty dollars later, the window was installed, and the girls were back in the saddle.

He'd given her a one hundred dollar bill for the job.

For the evening—I'm already ahead!

JoJo got out the taxi in front of *Los Banditos* around eleven p.m. The girls arrived an hour earlier to get ready and plan their routines.

She made it to the mall right before it closed. The Fila sweat suit and matching F-13s she had on, according to the enthusiastic salesgirl, were *"off the rack mean."* She opened the motorcycle club's door, anticipating a similar reaction. It'd only been a few months, but she loved the way men's clothing made her feel. Unlike her housemates, she could roll out of bed, wash her face, throw something on, and start her day. Short hair also meant never competing for mirror space. Adopting the look was the wisest decision she'd ever made. For the first time, she felt comfortable in her skin.

Except for a group shooting pool, the lounge was empty. She followed the music to the backroom, where she found Nella and Chanel.

The knotty pine paneled walls, parquet flooring and water-damaged drop ceiling were dated, but the space was clean, and warm. Next to a window, a radio sat atop a small table. She turned the volume down, and greeted them.

Chanel sat in front of a tall mirror, pressing an eyelash into position. JoJo tapped her on the shoulder. "Where's Foxy Roxi?"

"She went out back to smoke a j."

"By herself?"

"Yup."

Frustrated with a tangle in her fishnet stockings, Nella tossed the heap, into a bag on the floor. "Can't no body tell her nothing. She told us, she was good."

"I'm going to find her. Please be ready by the time I get back."

"All right, but I'm starving. I want a shot, but I haven't eaten since last night." Chanel turned around in the chair, and batted her eyes. "Can you get me something light?"

JoJo nodded her head. "I got you. No onions, tomatoes or hots, right."

"Right."

"What about you, Nella?"

"No thanks."

JoJo exited in search of Roxi, irritated she'd gone off on her own. None of them had even been in this place before. *Impressing Mr. Money Bags and making a good impression, should be her concerns. I hate that she takes so many stupid risks.*

The bartender stopped drying a glass when she approached. "Good evening. Have you seen a girl with blond hair?"

"Yeah–I think I saw ole girl go out back with Ro."

"Outback? How do I get there?"

"Walk past the pool tables, and turn down the hall. You'll see the grey door with the exit sign above it."

"Thanks."

She followed the directions, opened the door and stepped into a brightly lit patio. Foliage encased trellises, created a barrier around the perimeter. Replete with long picnic tables, seating areas, and an upcycled tank grill, she thought, *this place is perfect for entertaining.*

In the farthest corner, she made out two silhouettes. Though perturbed with the *simple* girl, Roxi's cackle was relaxing.

She interrupted Roxy mid-statement. "What's up?"

"Oh nothing. Ro had some dank and you know how I roll."

"Ro." JoJo noticed her coziness with the guy, she herself, just met. "I see."

Rohan tugged her elbow. "It's cool, Warden." He smiled. "We just shootin' the shit. What's up wit cha?"

"Nothing much. I just got here. Have I missed anything?"

"Not at all. We talked a lil bout how things usually go down. None of the particulars. Your timing's perfect. Let's go inside for a minute."

Roxi went in search of the girls, and JoJo took a seat at a table. Rohan joined her a few seconds later, holding Coronas with limes. "Thanks again for coming through in the crutch. Word. So let me put all my cards on the table—I know y'all new to town, but me and my brothers are well known, and been getting money for years. When we have some shit, we always get the big boys, the OGs—*yuuurd* me—out the house. We give these get-togethers for my niggas that don't stunt like they used to. Strip clubs are out of bounds. They fear getting robbed, kidnapped or worse. Lots of them got wifeys, so they're just looking for a little fun."

"Define fun?"

"You may get one or two that'll wanna suck some pussy, finger pop em, or ask for head. I'm not gonna bullshit you. But none of them want trouble. And if anybody gets out of line, my man Big Show, will deal with them." He slammed his fist into his palm for emphasis. "Nothing bad will happen on our watch."

"I'm listening." She loosened her jacket, and continued sipping the brew.

"You can do it how you want. It's your show, but I say give them a dance to get them interested in each girl. Then, they should come out, and do something together. After that, we can turn the lights down, and let em socialize. To the left of the bar is a small room. It's being tidied up, as we speak. Check it out when you have some time. What's it for? Use your imagination. Got any questions?"

"Everything makes sense, but I do have one…can lap dances start at twenty?"

"It's your world. We'll make sure everyone knows what's up. You tell us the rules, and we'll enforce them. Big man should be here shortly. He'll stay close to y'all, at all times. Any other questions, or requests?"

"Nah. I'm straight." He'd already explained, how they made their money wasn't his concern. She was ready to get the party started.

"I'm glad to hear. Here's two fifty for showing up."

Her eyes widened. "Thanks." She took the money and put it in her pocket.

"I told you I'd make this worth your while. You're helping me out more than you know."

"Tonight's celebration is for Big Paul from Perkins. He just came home. Man—his people are amped. Kicked out for catering, and magnums of Nectar. And asked me to have a stack of ones."

Cha Ching!

"I need to step out for a few. I'm picking up my little brother. He's coming home for the weekend. Give the DJ a list of songs that'll get the girls loose."

Get em loose, ha! Tonight's gonna be off the chain.

"I will. Where's he coming from, and how many brothers do you have?"

He chuckled. "A lot. There are seven of us, in total. No sisters, but my mother raised a few of my girl cousins. Scooter's a freshman at Virginia Tech. My family's proud. He's always been a real whiz kid."

"Six brothers—geez. Don't take this the wrong way, but mama was busy."

"No offense taken. I'm the oldest, so imagine how it was to watch them, keep coming, year after year. I stayed hungry when I was young because I made sure everyone else ate first." He beamed with the exuberance of a child. "I'll share more later on. Right now—I gotta get out of here. He's waiting at Penn Station."

"I'm cool. Do what you gotta."

Pointing to JoJo, he shouted before flying out the door, "Mr. Bill, I'll be back. Heading to grab Scoot. Listen for the back door. Get her anything she needs."

"Will do." Bill turned to JoJo. "You need anything before I go for ice?"

"Where's the best place, nearby, to get a bite to eat?"

"Roots. I'll call, and have someone bring whatever you like."

"Out of sight!"

25

LOS BANDITOS

"*L*adies and gentlemen, bros and hoes, OGs and everybody in between. Thank you for joining us for what we promise will be a pussy-filled I mean wonderful evening. Brian mawfuggin' Furst—my nigga. You ready for the bitches? Ooh Wee." Bingo, the host, kept it gully, and *hella* funny. Several in the horde cheered and yelled words of encouragement, loving his lack of subtlety. "Hell Yeah!"

"I want to give a special shout out to Peapot, who just finished a dime. You're looking good, my G. You got a shot coming, on me. What up, Scotty B! Some body get that man a drink. It's his birthday. I need the rest of y'all horny mahfuggahs to make your way to the front. Take it from me—we want her, and her sexy friends to come back. Please show some love for, Miss Vanilla."

Brunette with DDs, Nella marched to the center of the checkerboard dance floor with authority. Unbeknownst to everyone, rhythmic seduction was a specialty. While swaying around the square's perimeter, she removed her sparkly outfit, a piece at a time. She sauntered to the rear of the room, and returned with a fella for *"The Hot Seat."* So not to miss the action, those against the walls, stood on the tips of their feet.

With his hands by his sides, she stood behind his chair, and gave his meat a quick squeeze. While pretending to whisper in his ear, she ran her fingertips down his spine. Next, she stepped in front of him, bent over, and jiggled her ass. He smacked it.

She tossed her head back, licked her lips, and told him, "Stop it!" The crowd went wild.

As the song ended, he grabbed her wrist. "I'm tryna finish this. I want you on my lap, so bad." The bulge in his slacks was visible.

"I'll see you later." Continuing to moving sexily in front of him, she gathered her clothing, and the money tossed during the performance. "I'm not going anywhere. It's yours!"

The first act got the mob warmed up, but Roxi got them sizzling. By the time Chanel performed, men were ready to take a few liberties. Her entry alone, had a few ready to bone. She didn't have a choreographed number like the others, but she made her unveiling amazing.

A perk of private parties was girls got butt naked. Though illegal in licensed establishments, she worked out every day, and loved exhibiting her progress. Hot and sweaty from bouncing off the walls, she walked around, and let them inspect her work. In appreciation, bills of varying denominations, cascaded over her head.

After drying off, dressing, and downing a few clear shots, the trio mingled. The tips from dancing were nice, but *"one-on-ones"* were *"name your price."*

Chanel sat next to JoJo, and scoped out the *"possibilities."* Guys approached, and asked for her time, but she was holding out for a *"money maker."* A hopper in double denim slithered over. She sprang off the stool, and started massaging his shoulders. Evidently, he'd said something tempting. As she led him to the "green" room, his friends applauded his fortune. "Handle your business, yo."

When Chanel left, JoJo felt like all eyes were on her. Some wondered if she was the pimp or, *even wilder*, one of the dancers' girlfriend. By far, the biggest shock, since switching up her style, was the energy of women. There was a surprising number present. One, kept looking in her direction. While flattered, she wasn't curious, or moved by their directness.

A guy pulled out the adjacent stool, leaned over, and asked

what she wanted. "I'd rather not drink alone."

He was tall and super sexy, so she figured, *why not*. Wagering he wasn't a weirdo, she invited him to *"cop a squat."* The two-tone Tag Heuer, caught her eye. *Fresh Buttahs on his feet.* Though his gear was understated and he wore no gold, the Mercedes keys, and bump in his pocket, screamed dough.

She was enjoying the conversation, when Roxi moseyed over, and asked to be "introduced." Before responding, Rohan sat a bottle of 1738 on the bar in front of them. "Eh, lemme holla at you for a sec?"

"Sure." JoJo turned to Roxi. "I'll be back. Introduce yourself."

The duo waded through the crowd, and exited the front door. "Yo, I like how you and your girls roll. My dudes are saying this is the most fun they've had since The Underground and Odell's." He smiled at her perplexed looked. "Those were spots we used to shut down, back in the day. I forgot you're not from here. I bought you out here because I think we should do this again. How you feel about making it a regular thing."

"Sure. I like that idea. When are you thinking of starting."

"How about next Friday–Freaky Fridays."

"That's real creative."

"Not really. But it'll bring horny niggas out. We can charge what we want at the door, and I already got the Security. I see big things in the future. Fuck with the kid."

"Where though, cause this place ain't it. There's barely enough room for us to move around, as is. Also, I'm thinking we're gonna need more dancers to pull this off, and they're gonna need a place to change. A spot with a bathroom, just for us, would be ideal."

"Let me think on it. I got a few places in mind. Until then, start finding them girls. Let's talk some more tomorrow night."

"Sounds good to me."

By four a.m., the girls were dressed, and idling around the makeshift dressing room. JoJo tallied the money, but all had previously agreed, she could keep it. Curiosity about the final haul, kept them in suspense.

Roxi sat next to her. "When's the next one?"

"I don't know."

"I love going to clubs, and shaking my booty and tits. I love making paper too. This is the best of both worlds. I had a lot of fun."

"I'm meeting up with Rohan, tomorrow. Can I finish what I'm doing?" She also needed more time to think through the execution. The night was some hood shit— *janky squared*. They made money, but she knew they could do better. *If we got this much, out of this crowd, imagine what we could do, with planning. Cha Ching!*

"Cool. I'm ready. That muthafucker got crowded."

"Hell yeah," said Nella. "People must've gotten on the horn, and told people to come through."

One of the girls sparked a joint. Roxi moved closer to it. "Eh, Chanel, remember the old man in the brown leisure suit?"

"Oh, my gawd! Girl! Call him donkey dick. I ain't never seen nothing like it."

"Me either, but they say the dick and ears, never stop growing."

Nella stopped fiddling with her make-up kit. "Who?"

"The old ass man in the brown church suit. He couldn't keep his hands off Roxi."

She gagged. "Eww. I jerked his junk, but didn't go further than that. Not with him, anyway. Now—the cutie in the Adidas windbreaker…Yeah—he got it, and can get it again."

Nella interjected. "There were a number of lookers up in there."

"You ain't lyin'."

"The one in green, with the mouth full of golds…said his name was Tim. Gave me a hundred dollars to suck him off. I got my mouth real wet, heated these hands up real good, and went to town. You should've heard him, with his ole pepperoni pole,

'*Uuuuh, yeah baby…..Uuuuh baby, baby girl. Ahhhh!*'…he was done in two minutes flat. Ha! The mouth of the south strikes again."

Nella's colorful reenactment caused the girls to laugh raucously. JoJo loved their smiles, and prayed the peace lasted.

"Y'all see Mr. Bill?"

"Hell yeah, I ran into him." Chanel knew the perv, too well.

"He kept calling me, '*White lightening*'. I'm like – is that how you feel, Mr. Bill? Then he hit me with '*My daddy's been dead for twenty years. Call me Billy. You got my blood pumping. You better watch yourself.*' I never knew old men could be so frisky."

"Girl, his ass was something else—I swear fore gawd, you're the baddest bitch in here." Chanel imitated his inflection and tenor.

"He was in love, with all of us."

"Sure was."

JoJo laughed, but had nothing to contribute to the conversation. Listening to them trade notes on "tricks," like maids discussing stains, verified "disgusting" is subjective. Everyone is governed by a unique set of rules. For them, morality was a nonstarter. Paying bills meant taking no prisoners. *Who am I to judge?*

They needed the money desperately. Even with their low cost of living, she knew they needed to make *this kind of money*, regularly. Eating out and partying, as often as they did, was expensive. Rent was due on the first, and they already had a cut-off notice for the electric.

Rohan's opportunity, felt like a blessing. With the two he gave her, they were going home fourteen-hundred dollars richer.

"What's up with the guy that chit-chatted the shit out of JoJo all night," asked Roxi. "He was fine. I wonder if Rohan knows him."

"Yes, lardy. He was tall." Chanel yelled. "I stay away from them lanky niggas though. No thank you. They be tryna break a bitch in half."

"His name's Ish," said Nella. "We were supposed to hook up a while ago, but I never called him. I'm mad I didn't get a chance to holla at him, before he left. I think I still have his number. Shit!"

"Anyway. Let me get my shit together."

JoJo noticed Roxi's mood shift, and hoped to restore the camaraderie. "Twelve hundred and twenty-three dollars."

Chanel slammed the lid of her suitcase closed, and locked it. "Hell yeah. That's what I'm talking about!"

Nella thought it would've been more. "In the future, I'll pop my titties up, a little higher."

"That's the spirit!" JoJo wished they all shared her enthusiasm.

"Woo hoo! Now—can we go home?

"Yes, Roxi Rox. We're done. Time to go."

26

THE WOMEN OF MCELDERRY STREET

*C*hanel dumped a second cup of sugar into the pitcher, stirred, and took a sip. "Perfect." She put the Kool-Aid in the fridge, before resuming a Word Search. Normally, the exercise helped her unwind, but today, it provided nil release.

She hadn't been this ticked off in a while. Roxi *"borrowed"* a dress, then ruined it. *Lil bitch had the audacity to tell me where I got it from, and that she'd gimme my $14.99 back.*

"What the hell?" She asked herself aloud.

Roxi called her selfish, but for Chanel, fashion was freedom.

Sharing a pair of pants, and *too tight* shoes with four siblings, makes you value your own, when you get them. It'd been difficult acquiring the coats, dresses, hats, and heels, she'd amassed over the years, and she wouldn't allow another to damage or disrespect them. Regardless of how she felt on the inside, looking *sexy*, was a necessity.

I haven't reminded her in a while, so I'll give her a pass.

But, next time—I'ma get in that ass!

She'd never forget the day Shelly and her thirteen year old daughter, arrived at the house with a carload of trash bags. The adolescent's eye rolling and back talkin' were the first signs of trouble.

She caught her sucking Tank's dick in the bathroom one morning. Mortified, she stayed in her room, the rest of the day. She knew her man was a *dirty dog,* but she never had him liking kids.

With so many willing, of age participants—*Why destroy a life?*

She struggled to face both, until she learned Roxi was the pursuer. This confused her for a while, then at once, made sense. The impressionable girl, was all her *trifling, tattoo-ing, drug dealing, hooker mother/mentor*, prepared her to be. When the youngster started working with them, Chanel wasn't displeased. With Shelly gone, somebody had to buy Tank's Jack and weed. As it turned out, older men were her preference.

Chanel met Tank a few months after moving to Maryland. Compared to the man she'd escaped, the *sweet, funny guy* was a breath of fresh air. He worked at a tire shop, wore oversized duds, guzzled Mountain Dew, and ate ramen noodles daily, but his black Impala stayed waxed, and he treated her like a lady.

He also promised to be her ticket into the Rap industry. *"I've sold rims to lots of emcees and producers. Trust me. I can get you a hot track!"*

After repeatedly declining his invite to *"move in,"* she caved.

Tired of sleeping under bridges, but smart enough to avoid men saying the right things, she thought she'd found a king.

How could I've been so gullible?

His job laid him off, and everything changed. The jokes stopped, he drank more, and the household bills went unpaid. He wasn't a hustler by nature. Soon, his glow faded.

As proof of her dedication, she stepped up, and carried the weight. It was a small price to pay; he'd sheltered her when she was penniless, without a prayer.

In the beginning, *"hitting the streets"* was fun. They went to the popular hangouts. She got new clothes. He gassed her up; encouraged her to show off. *"Baby, you're a star."*

Bringing home money, and moving them in a positive direction, felt rewarding. Bit by bit, she got them on their feet. From the outside looking in, their arrangement made little sense, but nothing diminished her glee. She blocked out what she did with other men. Buying his clothes, liquor, bud, and filling up the ride, filled her with pride. Her eyes were locked on the prize.

For all his bull crap and bluster, no one took advantage, and he kept her safe. He was the only person beating her. He didn't do it often; usually when he was drunk. If she ignored the signs of a looming explosion, she blamed the bruises on herself. Much of what he threw in her face was stuff she'd told him. All that withstanding— it wasn't until Tank met Shelly, that she accepted, the loser meant her no good.

Do I miss him? Some days—but those were far, and few. He was her past. She couldn't wait until the same could be said about *crazy ass* Biz.

In the beginning, they hooked up on the late night tip or when she was bored. Things were easy and breezy. He was new, cute, and convenient. She looked forward to sleeping with the freaky pleaser. His bringing skunk, didn't hurt, either. She didn't smoke often, but when she did, she wanted to blow the best. Fucking around with guys from *"up top,"* she'd developed a preference for hydro. *"Brown"* or anything with twigs and seeds was *"dirt,"* and thus, unacceptable. *Yes!*—It was that serious.

If allowed, Biz could eat the *"beaver"* for hours. Eveready, he never complained. With a dick the size of a plantain, her nether region ached for days.

Two months later—he's fascinated by how she paid her bills. On top of the questions about who she *"dated,"* he begged to hear all the raunchy details. Some of their conversations led to the most intense sex, for both.

Far more skilled in the carnal arts, she introduced him to sensations he'd never known. Assuming they were on the same page, she continued, *"sucking his soul out of his holes."*

His prior bravado faded, and she hated the submissiveness that replaced it. The boundless energy disappeared too. He no longer slurped her till she squirted, without her agreeing to his annoying stipulations. Finger fucking him, while sucking him off, turned him completely out. When he started wanting *strap in the ass action*, more than back shots, she knew they were through.

"You a fag?" The question sent him ballistic.

After clearing her dresser top, he called her everything, but a child of God, and aggressively threatened to, *"split her wig to the white meat!"*

Chanel seized the basement when Nella joined them, and ordinarily, appreciated the privacy. Though on this occasion, the close quarters felt confining.

She asked him to remove himself from her presence, and never speak to her again. He mumbled a few things under his breath, but left without incident. All was calm for a few weeks, then random shit started happening.

Tank ensured men never got too close. That's not to say she felt JoJo could've done anything to stop him. She didn't tell her about the drama, hoping the shit storm, quickly passed.

If it wasn't for bad luck, I wouldn't have any.

JoJo was one of the realest people she'd met in a long time, but Chanel called her a *"smart dummy."* Kind hearted and bookish as hell, but unable to see the vultures and vampires swarming around her.

She had far bigger concerns than creating an air of serenity.

Roxi preyed on her kindness, and as far as she was concerned, *White Lightening* moved *too* quietly.

If only the people back home could see me now thought Nella as she stood in the *Total Male* checkout line for Hardy. He'd been on the phone since they arrived, but she was used to his detachment. Since she was on his shit list, she played the humble helper. It wasn't glamorous, but she tolerated the hazing without complaining. He was an asshole of the first order, but rewarded her for enduring his moods.

Baltimore was a big city compared to Forsyth County, Georgia. In the beginning, she wasn't sure she could survive. The utopian dream she'd hatched in a tire swing, quickly turned to a nightmare. The guy she'd given a deposit for an apartment, turned out to be a scammer. She couch surfed for weeks, until a sweet lady, she met at *Social Services*, offered a spare room.

Miss Dotty worked the nightshift, which meant she often had the huge house to herself. There was always food and cable TV, which suited doe-eyed *Bethany Haskell*, just fine.

Nella and her son Joaquin, or Jolly as everyone called him, were two trains passing in the night. He ran the streets 24/7, and paid her little attention.

She assumed.

Six months after moving in, one rainy afternoon, he cornered her. *"Do you like me?"*

She'd fantasized about being his girl, the first time she saw him. On many nights, she'd swayed herself to sleep, imagining him between her legs. This was her chance to gain a dream come true. *"Of course."*

"Good." She smiled at the memory. *He was so arrogant!*

Hoping a girlfriend would inspire him to do better, his mother gave them her blessing. She was thrilled to have bought them together.

The perfect gentleman, Joaquin showed her how a man treats a woman, for whom he has noble intentions. Her affection and concern, made him strive to reach higher levels. He stopped running with Hardy, which caused tension between the best friends. Together every day since third grade, he couldn't understand why Jolly let her get into his head.

Money flowed slowly, but he celebrated outwitting the streets. Square living wasn't lucrative, but peace beat ducking and dodging hooks and crooks, or getting dragged into beef.

A job cleaning carpets, inspired him to buy his own equipment. The business was still new, but many of his customers referred friends.

Their relationship was stronger than ever when he was murdered, walking home from the bank. They later learned, a teen gang banger shot him, to gain a higher rank.

In the aftermath, Hardy lent an unwavering hand of support

to the family. Miss Dotty never liked him, but accepted to his condolences. She initially resisted his *"financial assistance,"* but Nella persuaded her to listen.

Following the somber repast, he proposed, going for a drive. She agreed, happy to get some air. He took her to secluded waterway in Severn nestled behind a row of stately homes. It made for a perfect escape, from the melancholy of the day.

He parked the Supra on a gravel lot, and they walked to the end of a long landing. Ahead, another couple was in the process of leaving. The men nodded to one another. *"Take it easy."* Mute retirees, sat along the shoreline, and fished. It was dark, but they were minding their business.

Hardy pulled her close, and led them to a hidden patch of sand. They looked up and admired the moon, until the wind gust grew stronger. He offered his jacket, which smelled of Drakkar Noir. Jolly wore the same cologne. It was an aphrodisiac.

Until that night, she'd never noticed Hardy had waves, or that his lips were so tempting. She couldn't stop imagining how they'd feel on her nipples. As hard as she tried, the longer they sat, the more she wanted to make love. She was starving, having never gone, so long, without warmth. Though it was immoral on many levels, Hardy felt safe. As if he sensed she needed it, he pulled her closer, and she rested her head on his chest.

When they got back to the car, Nella tugged at his zipper, and grabbed the keys, stopping him from sticking them in the ignition. His dick and semen, tasted sweet going down her throat. With her eyes closed, she imagined Jolly, giving her both.

In the ensuing months, they screwed nearly every night. Whenever and wherever he wanted, she never declined, or put up a real fight. Hardy did things Jolly respected her too much to request. He was sadistic, freaky, defied her limits, and pushed her to glorious heights.

Miss Dotty discovered their trysts, and posthaste obtained an order of eviction.

Nella thought they'd take their connection to the next level.

Instead, he gave her a twelve hundred dollars, and told her, *"Holla when you need that box battered."* In addition to losing her refuge and tie to her soul mate, she also lost a true friend.

Scraping by in her adopted town, forced her to shed her conservative views. Heartbroken and homeless, she turned to boosting. In the early days, it was department stores, then she graduated to higher end boutiques. Trusting salespersons, afforded her the privilege of privacy. She eventually mastered paystubs, and doctoring titles. With ease, she strolled into dealerships, and left with the car or boat she wanted, after answering a few questions.

Sad reality—talent is only valuable if you get paid for it.

That's when Hardy came back in the picture. His assistance was the thing she wanted but, he buffered her from risk. His endorsement and reputation, stopped hooligans and impostors from being disrespectful.

Hardy was a freak without limits. She was trained for every sexual scenario. He opened her eyes to a new lane, but treated her like an idiot. *"Work smarter not harder. Stop putting yourself at risk."*

All of her shoes and clothes were hand-picked. He told the stylist how to streak her hair. Educated her on perfumes, lotions, dark mascara, leather bags, and how to spot expensive jewelry. He also taught her how to remain relevant.

Maintaining her lifestyle required a consistent stream of coinage. Her days were spent staying thick fit, smelling sweet and collecting compliments. An hour on curls and another on makeup were normal.

He taught her people who claimed, *"I don't see color,"* are full of shit. Too many men adored her and gave her money because of it. Black men were always curious about what made her different. Mutually intrigued, she aimed to be the insatiable sex pot, most believed, white girls to be.

"Seize every opportunity. Give them niggas the business!"

Her trust was explicit. She followed his guidance, without misgivings.

She stumbled into a world where being herself was money in the bank. The same voice, figure, and cultural preferences, that once made her a pariah, now, made her exotic.

They'd made lots of money, but she was tired of the lies, the empty promises, and wiping tears from her eyes. She'd long stop caring whether they'd be a couple. When the infatuation faded, she knew she could do better. He manipulated her self-doubt, and weaponized her insecurities.

He complained about who she'd become.

"I made you! Neva forget. I remember when your accent was thick."

He'd met before she ditched the glasses, and got her teeth fixed. The shy girl who only wanted love, bubble gum, and cum.

In a city where showing love isn't rewarded, she was a darling among hustlers, and hitmen. All the bad bitches, coke boys, and top-tier promoters, wanted her at their events.

Every scam was the last. Proving she had grit, or the desire for praise, were no longer compelling motivations. Respect was her primary need, and he wouldn't give it.

She found him snoring, with a young chick, tucked under him. It hurt. *Why didn't he take her to a hotel?* Fury engulfed her. After flushing an eighth of a key, she slapped both of them awake, and got out of there before he came to his senses.

JoJo's offer to *"move-in,"* answered her prayers. She needed a place to lay low, that wasn't in West Baltimore. Unsure if hitters were stalking, she kept away from the usual haunts.

Instead of an angle to exploit, the uninitiated *newbies* made her feel important. Money flowed without assistance, but she enjoyed showing them the ropes.

When she saw Hardy months later, he told her she was beautiful, and ordered her a drink. She slipped into his lap and kissed him, savoring his woodsy aftershave.

"You owe me."

"I know."

"Big. I don't want no shit out of you when it's time to pay me back."

She would've agreed to anything he asked to get out of the

club unscathed. Later that night, she went back to what used to be their place. He threw her across their bed. The sex was sweaty, rough, and electric. It was everything that made his particular brand of manipulation effective.

Afterwards, he pulled her closer, wrapped his muscular arms around her waist, and snored like a freight train. Though she'd slept in thousands of hotel rooms, thinking of the stories her *old* mattress held, kept her wide awake.

"Fuck you doing?" snapped Hardy.

His attitude, startled her. "What do you mean?"

"The line's moving, and you're just standing there. Come on. Are you with me or what?"

"I don't even know what you're talking about. You've ignored me since you picked me up. Why are you fussing? There's a person in front of us."

"You're funny as shit. You ought to be happy to be with me, at all."

"Yeah—whatever."

"Don't whatever me. You're lucky."

He smiled, but she didn't find anything humorous. She looked straight ahead, not wanting things to turn unruly.

"Why did you look away? I'm fucking with you. Turn around—Let me see your face." She obeyed. "I was hollerin' at my main man about something we're tryna put together. I'm sorry you feel ignored."

"Okay."

"I may need your help."

"Help with what?" He had a way of making her do things she regretted later.

"I'll tell you more, once I iron out a few things. Right now, I'm tryna find out what I gotta do to get you to come back home."

"For what?" Until he valued all she brought to the table, beyond money, that was out of the question. She loved him, but didn't trust his motives.

After brushing a tendril from her eye, he gently touched the tip of her nose. "I miss you. I know you miss me too."

"I don't believe you." He pulled her closer. Her heart pumped faster.

"How bout we stop by Pretty Please when we leave here, and I'll show you."

She smiled seductively. "I'd like that."

Roxi sprinted to the clinic entrance to avoid the downpour. She placed her coat over a chair before registering. An older Caucasian women in pink scrubs, handed her a clip board of papers. "Fill them out, and hold on to them until your name is called."

She didn't know much about her family, and it was impossible to calculate her number of *"lifetime partners."* After filling in what she felt was important, she sat back and mentally prepared for the appointment. She grabbed a Magazine from the nearby stand, sat down, and tried to suppress her anxiety.

A week earlier, she noticed two red bumps in her pubic area above her clitoris. She dismissed them as ingrown hairs, after hastily shaving with a dull razor. Twelve hours later, a fissure appeared near her anus, and a cluster of fluid-filled blisters covered part of her labia. These were sore to the touch, really itchy, and burned like hell when she peed. Several days of pain and stress passed before the pain brought her to her knees.

Children gleefully ran circles around the packed waiting room. An enormous aquarium, colorful train set, and toy chest, told her their presence was normal.

A few girls were there with their boyfriends. Looks of grief and shame told her some were there for abortions. Posters on endoscopic pregnancies, IUDs, vaccines for HPV, and other diseases covered the powder blue walls. None of it was comforting. She felt ready to cry.

Five minutes later, a door opened, and a brunette in a lab coat appeared. "Rochelle Hudgens."

"Over here." She grabbed her coat and approached.

"Good afternoon. My name is Peggy. How are you today?"

"I'm okay. Should I give this to you?"

"Yes—thank you." The smiling woman took the medical history forms.

"Are you the doctor?"

"No. I'm the nurse practitioner performing your exam."

"Oh—okay."

Roxi followed her to a small, brightly lit room. The nurse retrieved a paper gown from a drawer, and instructed her to disrobe. "Everything from the waist down. I'll be back, in a few minutes."

When the door closed, Roxi took off everything save her socks. She looked at the white walls, and outside of a few English countryside prints, the place felt sterile and cold. A few minutes later, Peggy returned carrying a tray laden with utensils and tubes.

"Have you ever had a pap smear, Rochelle?"

"No."

"Okay. I'm going to ask you to get on the table. Then, you'll put your feet in the stirrups. I'll insert a speculum to open you up, so I can't get a look. From there, I'll collect a few samples. There may be a little discomfort, but it'll be over relatively quickly. I reviewed your forms, and noted swelling and painful lesions. Is that your primary reason for visiting?"

"Yes."

"I'll swab any I see, and send them off for full testing. For now, I'll take a look under the microscope. Do you have any questions before we get started?"

"No."

"You can go on, and hop up on the table then."

"Okay." Roxi took her time. It hurt like hell to move. She reclined, and put her heels into the metal cups. Though she bathed before leaving the house, her vagina smelled like rot. She considered apologizing, but mortification stopped her.

The nurse sat down, wheeled a stool closer, and flicked on a fluorescent light. Accustomed to noxious odors, she focused on her work, without fright. "Concentrate on the butterflies, on the ceiling. It'll be over, before you know it." She put on latex gloves, and examined the outer folds of her vagina. Next, she lubricated two fingers, stood, and inserted them. After pressing down a few times on Roxi's abdomen, she inquired about her level of pain. "I'm fine."

"Great." She sat down again, and retrieved the speculum from the tray. From this position, she couldn't see much, which made the experience more unsettling. Roxi winced when the metal device was inserted. "Everything okay?"

"Yes. I felt a chill."

"Sorry about that. You may feel a slight pinch, as I collect a specimen for the lab." With each twist and click, the pressure increased, as her cervix widened. "Take deep breaths and relax. You may feel some pressure, but there shouldn't be any pain. If you do, let me know."

She felt the brush's long bristles rake her interior walls. A few seconds later, the nurse removed the tool, but told her not to move. She wiped her lady parts with a moist cloth before directing her to sit up. "All done."

After collecting the slides, she left Roxi alone again. She grabbed a few paper towels from the dispenser, and carefully wiped away the remaining goo. She was tying her laces when Peggy announced what she'd suspected.

"It looks like you have Herpes Simplex II, dear, but I won't be certain until the results come back. Don't worry yourself. It's common." She gave her a pamphlet on how to prevent the spread. "There's medicine you can take to lessen the pain, and frequency of outbreaks. Unfortunately, there's nothing available to completely stop them. Patients say ice, and Tylenol or Advil helps. Keep your stress level low, and use latex prophylactics."

She then handed her a prescription for meds to treat trichomonas. "You'll need to take all of the antibiotics. The odorous discharge should decrease in a few days."

Roxi smiled.

Somewhat pleased, she left weighing her obligation to share the diagnosis with her current lovers. Country and Keefy hit it raw—*on the regular*, and neither would be sympathetic.

27

PLUMB DUMB

*R*oxi woke up in a piss poor mood. As usual, she complained about things that couldn't be changed. Normally, everyone ignored her rants, but Gus fed into the bullshit.

JoJo thought, *why?*

"Our biggest competition is those skuzzy ass ball fifty bitches. I keep hearing niggas talk about them. I ain't never bumped into nare one of them. Clearly, we don't even travel in the same circles."

He lit a beedi. "I know all them broads. Most of them from down the hill. Ain't nobody checking for that raggedy puss. All of East Baltimore, done run through em." After a few inhales he continued, "But on some real shit **sssss** **sssss** fuck them. Y'all got something they don't have."

"What?"

"A whooty woo—a white girl with a booty."

Nella smiled.

"Plus, y'all got JoJo."

Roxi rolled her eyes, then glared at Nella. "I'm not worried about them. They can keep trickin' for kicks and shrimps, I want top dollar for my talents. Ya girl's the one fucking up the aesthetic."

Nella slammed the magazine she was reading on the table, and looked at JoJo. "This hoe always saying something smart. You better get her."

"I know you think your ass is all that, but you ain't gotta

have them floppy titties, and lumpy cheeks, hanging out! I can't believe some of the shit you wear. Those skanky ass outfits you love, scream—cheap."

JoJo gasped, in disbelief. *Girl! You're always talking shit!*

"I really wanna know, who she thinks, she is?"

"You know who I am. Talk to me. Don't talk about me. Who the fuck do you think you are?"

"A bossy bitch with supreme clientele. Who keeps her hair, nails, and toes, done. There's always a few stacks in my Louie bag, and according to your boy Ish, I taste good too."

"*Mmk*—a bossy bitch with supreme clientele. Ha! You're corny, as shit. Fuck outta here! Those bottom dwellers you fuck wit out Curtis Bay and Brooklyn got you gassed. You're regular degular as shit. Sit your ass down. And don't say shit to me about Ish. He's only after you because you're (*air quotes*) different."

"I'm sick of your shit, Roxi! I'm White. So what! Is that all you got? Fuckin' one trick pony. We're in the same goddamn boat. You ain't no better than me. I ain't no better than you. Keep the racist bullshit up, and I'ma show you this white girl ain't no chump."

"You ain't finna do shit!"

"Stop pump faking! One day, you're gonna mess around and threaten the wrong person."

"*Ohhhh!* You hear her, JoJo?"

"Nah—this between me and you!"

"She really don't know."

Nella turned red. With flared nostrils and clenched fists, she looked at the taller girl defiantly. "Jump bitch! We can do this, if you feelin' froggy!"

Buurp Buurp! Buurp Buurp!

"That's Country. Consider yourself lucky." Roxi grabbed her purse from the counter.

"Lucky? Whatever." Nella was amped for a fight.

Roxi laughed. "Jump!"

"Little girl, don't let the hue fool you."

JoJo wanted to strike, both of them. One, for being a mean

girl, and the other, for taking the bait. "Y'all talking crazy! Please, stop! I'm done. Roxi, don't forget about the party in the county. I don't know where we're going, so be here by eight, at the latest."

"No worries. You might need to write it down for that one over there though. She likes to disappear for days without explanation. Betta make sure she'll be around."

Buurp Buurp! Buurp Buurp!

"I don't have to explain..."

"Forget all that you're talking. I've got to go! JoJo, I'll be here."

"Thank you."

When the door slammed shut, JoJo considered how to smooth things over. Both were iron-willed and egotistical, and neither eagerly embraced counterviews. She was no stranger to power struggles, but their bickering had reached an unsustainable level.

"Nella, you two don't like each other. We all get it—oil and water don't mix. I stay outta the drama. Y'all grown, but I'ma need you to be the bigger person. Knock it off. End it."

"Me? Explain. I go out of my way to avoid that bi-polar girl. I'm about my paper. You see how I get down. The real question is—what's her deal?"

"Maybe it's jealousy."

"Why though? She's fine. Guys tell her all the time."

"Girl, black people got lots of complexes. One of them is complexion."

"I understand. I've heard this before, but it's not 100% clear."

"Well—before you came along, Roxi was the light bright in the crew."

"She still is. I'm Scots Irish—White as they come."

"You and I understand, but she sees you as a threat. You stole her thunder." JoJo found it ironic people obsessed over Nella being white. *Merle's a shade lighter.* She also suspected Roxi's ire stemmed from the imagined chance with Ish, but didn't mention it.

Nella believed Chanel and Roxi were prettier, with better bodies, but *the heart wants what it wants.* She exhaled and scratched her head. "Well—that's plumb dumb as my Me-maw used to say." Following an extended pause she concluded, "I don't know how to make that better."

"Therein, lies the problem. She's immature. Only time can fix that. You be the bigger person. See things for what they are."

"Bigger person? I swear….some people. We're on the same team. I'm not her competition."

"I know."

"This has been happening to me since grade school. People are still mad at me, for the way God made me. I'm sick of it, but I think I get it."

"Hold up! Hold up!" Gus leaned forward, laughing and slapping his knee. "Neeva one of y'all gonna say nothin about Me-maw?"

"Boy, shush!"

"Mind your business."

"Thanks, JoJo. You've actually helped a lot. I feel a million times better. I can't lie and say I understand completely, but I trust your judgement. From now on, I'm going to try my best to walk away."

"I'm glad. That's all I can ask. For the record, I'm not saying you should turn down your shine."

"You're right about that. I'm going to go figure out what I'm wearing, then I'll probably take a nap."

"That's what's up. I'm heading out in a bit myself. I'll get up with you later."

"All right." Nella walked up to JoJo and hugged her. "Thank you." She lifted her skirt hem, and strolled across the room. "Bye, Gus."

"Peace out. Eh—don't let these hoes get you worked up."

JoJo had forgotten he was present. He'd been dismissed when he let his thirst for Nella slip.

"I'll see you later, too."

"Why?"

"I'm still putting pieces together for later, and need to holla

153

at a few people."

"See—I thought you were gonna stop doing that."

"Doing what?"

"Zoning out. Living inside your head. Don't block me out of your thoughts."

"I have no thoughts, outside of getting ready for work."

"Yeah—Ard." He stood and stretched, revealing his ripped abs. "Call me when you get in."

"I will." His physique turned her on, but it would take more than sex appeal to get back in her bed.

"Can I get a hug, or kiss before I go?"

He still don't get it! "Not right now."

He turned his cap to the back. "These streets are mean."

"Be careful, out there."

"It's like that?"

She gave him a two finger salute. "Peace."

"Don't be like that."

"Like what?"

"Stop acting hard, when you aren't."

She didn't respond.

"I'll let myself out."

"Be sure to set the bottom lock."

"That's cool. I see how you're carrying it. Good bye."

"Toodles." *Of all people, he should've known better.*

She prized loyalty over everything. Without it, they had nothing. His candidly sharing he'd checked out Nella's ass, hurt like a cheap shot.

He'd fuck her, if given the chance. Fine! But why flirt in my face?

Instead of the boss he always told her she was, he left her feeling basic. She still slept with him occasionally, but that was a matter of proximity, and ease. He also didn't grumble about her availability or wearing condoms.

All that said, I'll cut him off without regret, if he plays dumb again.

28

ISH

*F*ridays on the 400 block of *East Baltimore Street* were poppin'. Music blasting. LED lights flashing. Hustlers mackin'. Some trappin'. Drunk suburbanites yelling, and crudely laughing, at those passing. Tikes on bikes ducking sedans, circling in search of easy action. Sassy tramps stroked egos and patted sweaty backs, while promising to do something nasty.

A few hundred sailors had spilled out of their ship, and into the downtown dens of deviance and splendor. After months at sea, even the streetwalkers, looked tempting.

Someone sounded the alarm on the invasion of succors with money to tip. She'd already seen a few who'd claimed this was a *"bum bitch strip."* Time in the trenches taught her, hunger tests one's mores. And—*if you need it bad enough, you'll do the deed, and reflect on your morals in the morning.*

A year before, standing there, as she was, would've been inconceivable—*outside the Foxy Lady, facing Central District, smoking dank, feeling gangsta as shit!* With her middle finger in the air she thought, *fuck the law! Fuck all y'all! S*he laughed out loud. *I need to stop bumping so much Pac.*

In reality, this wasn't the place to be self-righteous. *Wolves are always lurking.* She only had an hour to find a few *baddies* ready to twerk. Given the time crunch, a *poon smorgasbord* was ideal.

The guy she'd drank shots with at Banditos, was getting out

of a CLK coupe. Rohan told her, he was his brother Tummy's homeboy, and came to all their events.

He has the hots for Nella. This should be interesting.

Ish walked up to her with a big smile on his face. Compared to the average man, he was a giant. At 5'9 and 6'4, they made a curious-looking pair. His Houston Rockets jersey and khaki shorts, accentuated his broad shoulders, muscled arms, and strong legs.

"What up, homie."

She gave him a hug. "Not much. It's Ish—right?"

"Yup, and you're JoJo."

"In the flesh. You remembered."

"I'm pretty good with names."

"Did you get taller since I last saw you?"

"Nah. You shrunk a few inches."

"You've got jokes. Wassup with them joints you're wearing?" She pointed to his feet. She'd never seen wine-red Air Force-1s with bubble gum soles. *I wondered if they're custom.*

"My tennis? You like these?"

"Hell yeah!"

"We buy 'em by the case. You gotta go to Rudo's or Cinderella's up Park Heights. They sell shit you don't see nowhere else. B'more put these on the map. We love em. As for these—we had to buy 100 pairs."

"That's some boss shit! The broads though, love their deekey Rees."

"Yes they do!"

"What about you?"

"I don't discriminate."

"I heard that. You drinking?"

"I'm down, but I gotta take it easy."

"Yeah? Whatever. Come on, I got you."

The twosome went into the establishment, and took seats at the bar, with their backs to the action.

"What are you doing down here this early?"

"Ion know. I like it down here during the day. Some of those old heads are real charmers. They show love…make my drinks right. What's your excuse?"

"We got a party later. I'm down here looking for girls."

"Oh word. So…."

A bartender interrupted his thought. "What can I get you?"

"You call it. What we sipping on?"

"I'll take a Goose and cranberry. I'm tryna stay away from that dark shit. Man—I become a different person."

"I feel you on that." He laughed. "My dudes fuck with brown heavy, but I'm with you. So yeah Miss, I'll have the same thing. Now—finish telling me about tonight."

"Ion know him, but everything seems official."

The woman returned with their drinks, and both thanked her. JoJo clanked her glass with Ish's before taking a sip.

"Eh sweetie, you mind settling up. I apologize, if you wanted to start a tab, but my shift bout to end."

"No problem." He pulled a twenty from the top of his knot. "Keep the change."

"Thank you, boo!"

"Now—back to you. Whose party is it?"

"Some dude from the county named Greg Coates. He drives a Viper. The cousin who booked us, was at an event we did at the Red Door a few weeks ago. I haven't the slightest idea what we're getting ourselves into, but he paid the deposit, so we'll be there."

"I ain't heard about it, so I must not know em."

"I wouldn't be surprised. From what I've seen, city and county mofos, do little mingling." She swirled the mixture around with a finger. "They're getting a whole nother level of money out there. No one posts up on the block or stands on a strip. Most of em bang off pagers, serving white fiends, and SSI recipients. I expect big things, but never mind all that though— what's up with you? We never got around to talking about the kind of stuff, besides sneakers, you like? You ball?"

"I shoot around, pickup games at the Dome or Cloverdale,

from time to time. Nothing major. I hear And-1 spose to be bringing the league to different cities. If it happens, I'm sure my man will put a dream team together. I'd be down to play."

"That's sounds nice, and it'd be a win for the city."

"Yeah—it would, if niggas act like they got some sense."

JoJo closed her eyes, and bobbed her head, in agreement. "You ain't lying about that. Shit's wild. What else?"

"Other than that, I like ordinary shit. Movies, go carts, cruisin', and shootin' dice with my boys."

"I don't get out much. My weekends are usually pretty busy. That's when I make my money. Baltimore is nothing like Miami, or DC. It's a lot easier to find trouble, than fun."

"Word. DC—is that where y'all from?"

"Yes and No. I'm from the District, Roxi and Chanel were living in PG when I met them, and we bumped into Nella across the street."

"Oh yeah, that's wassup. I, for one, love Chocolate City. I've been to a few of y'all clubs. I was up in Live, a few weeks ago. I've shopped in Georgetown a few times. Ate at Houston's. And the broads—good god! So many flavors to choose from."

"There is definitely more shit to get into, and I know what you mean about the women." She really didn't, but wanted to sound cool.

"My birthday's coming up, and I haven't figured out what to get into. I'm turning 23. I was thinking about going someplace, but I don't do planes, and road trips ain't my steez either. A party would be nice, but I don't have the time, and wouldn't know where to start, planning something like that."

Their birthdays were days apart, but she kept the conversation focused on him. *Everyone in the house has a hustle. It's time I join the club.* The fourteen-karat gold rope on lay-a-way, wasn't going to pay for itself. She'd become more dependent on *the girls*, who consistently brought home less dough. A party could be the life preserver, she knew they needed to stay afloat.

He was a *'whale'* as Merle would say, and his co-sign,

guaranteed her name recognition increased. *It's time for something big!* Her bank balance was anemic.

Her shopaholic roommates rubbed off on her in undeniable ways. When your appearance is everything, it's hard to plan for rainy days. New caps, watches, and sneakers depleted more and more of her funds weekly.

Before fear got the better of her, she divulged her thoughts. "Sounds like you need some help. Let me throw your bash. You won't regret it. I'd consider it an honor, and I promise, it'll be all that."

"Word—you'd do that?" He'd heard a lot of positive things about her from a variety of sources. There wasn't any doubt in his mind, her willingness was his good fortune.

"Sure. I'll make sure it's an extravaganza. Paul at *Rodeo*'s, been tryna get me to take a night. Have you been there since they remodeled?"

"Nah."

"It's nice. Half the spot is VIP. He re-did all the bars. Put in a new sound system, lights, smoke machines, and all. Full kitchen, and plush seating, too. Shit's hot."

"*Ard*—let's do it. I'm sold! I don't want you to skimp on anything. This needs to be some top flight shit. My niggas gonna be rolling with me, so it's gotta be platinum plus—*yuuurd me*. How much you need to get started?"

JoJo loved that he was so enthused. She hadn't known what to expect, but was glad she'd spoke truth to power. "I don't know. Off the top of my head—maybe a couple hundred for flyers and tickets."

"That's it? Cool."

"I hear they call you Mr. B'more."

Ish peeled off four hundred dollars, and sat it on the bar. "Yeah right. Don't nobody love me, but my mama. But on the real—this bout to be the shit."

"I love it!"

"Let's bring the city out! Take my math. Hit me when you

lock in a date. I'll tell all my people."

"Here." She handed her a black and gold calling card. "This is for you. Write your number on the back of this one for me."

"Look at you—a professional."

"I try."

"Here ya go. If you don't mind, I'd like to switch subjects. Wassup with your girl?"

"Which one?"

"Nella."

She put the card he marked in her back pocket. "She's around. Call her."

Ish tilted his head back, and laughed. When JoJo noticed the time, she stood, and pointed to her watch. "Thanks again, for the drink and opportunity. I'll call you soon. I've spotted a few of the people I need to see."

"You're welcome. Do that. I'm waiting on you."

"Eh, Brit! Hold up," yelled JoJo, after jetting away.

29

HUNNIT PROOF

*F*or JoJo's birthday, Rohan paid for a spa day. He picked her up, and dropped her off, under the entrance awning. The opulent *Turf Valley Country Club* reminded her of places she'd accompanied Merle during her youth. Inviting from the reception, she felt enthused.

A cheerful blond with a booty, offered a robe and led her to a dressing room. "When you're finished, leave your garments in a locker. I'll be waiting for you."

Ooh, la la—the deluxe package, included a full body peel, Shiatsu massage, and a mani/pedi. She tipped the masseuse, *Leslie*, extra. Whispering as she exited, "*Your touch is heavenly.*"

Over too soon, she dressed, feeling refreshed. She couldn't wait to get home, and take a nap.

His silver G Wagon awaited her emergence from the building. The interior glowed. Outkast boomed from the speakers when she opened the door. He lowered the volume. "You look furred."

"I am."

"And you deserve it. I keep telling you to take better care of yourself."

"I will. Today was the shit. I see me doing this again."

"And you should. You're the hardest working person I know."

"Thank you again."

"Don't mention it." He pointed to the ashtray. "Spark! That's you."

"You don't have to tell me twice. Thank you again, for everything. Where would I be without you?"

"I can't imagine." He laughed, turned the music up, and pulled away from the curb.

She glanced at him bobbing his head, and thought *If only you knew*. The butter soft seats, had never felt so lush. Smoking had been on her mind for hours—*and he came through with da sour!* She slipped off her shoes, rubbed her feet over the plush mats, and savored the flavor.

He smiled and shouted over the bass. "How you love that? Good, right?"

After successive pulls, she admired the roll with chinky eyes. "Irie."

By most assessments, Rohan wasn't aesthetically pleasing. He was fat, dark as coal with a big nose, and soup cooler lips, but exuded the confidence of Prince Charming. He was larger when they met, but lost eighty pounds, after switching to a pescatarian diet. His wavy coils were longer on the top and faded above his ears. Gaultier Le Male and Irish Spring, blended to create, his distinct scent. In the time she'd known him, he'd never repeated an outfit.

If she were looking for a boyfriend, he'd be at the top of the list. Though he never made advances, an intense attraction developed over time. He needed only to hint at interest, and she would've consented.

He praised her appearance, but never defiled her with his eyes. She considered giving him a glimpse of her girlier potential, but chickened out every time.

Let's be real. At this point, it'd be cross-dressing.

He was all man, but didn't mention, or look at women in her presence. His faithfulness to his wife and children, made him more endearing.

Privacy was paramount. There were those, whose come-up plan, started with taking off his head. As they bonded, Rohan let her into his world. He netted 40K a month via collections, poker parties, gift cards, and rent-a-wrecks, but knockoff electronics were his meat and potatoes. How he acquired the things he peddled, left JoJo scratching her head.

With his mother and sisters, he also owned several brick and mortar *"cash cows"*—a dry cleaners/laundromat, and a famed hair salon. JoJo was one of the few who'd seen his Woodstock (Baltimore County) farm. Gaining his trust, felt like a triumph.

Making friends, has never been easy. Her line of work, and sexual preference, in light of her presence, confused women and alpha men. He accepted her as she was, and never questioned her sovereignty.

She meant it when she told him she loved him.

When he returned the sentiment, she believed him.

Wise beyond his years, when he wasn't schooling her on the pitfalls of success, they discussed living on one's own terms. On free days, they cruised, bumped Project Pat, smoked, and reflected on what it meant to be American. Between lights, he pointed out former hangouts, places he'd lived, and properties he hoped to own.

He knew every corner of the city—from the main streets to the cuts, who was *gettin' money*, and those down on their luck. He imagined—*"Charm city's changing for the better!"*

If not for him, she wouldn't have known.

It was just as run down as it was when she arrived, but saying so would've been rude. He adored his hometown so she opened her mind, and focused on the potential.

"I'm in these streets. Best part—most times I play the middle man. That's how I get it, coming a thousand different ways. Anybody saying there's no bread in the hood is lying or dumb. Shiiid, the underground economy's the reason there isn't more homelessness."

She learned the *After-Hours* was for Rohan, and his friends to have fun. The earnings enabled them to keep the good times rolling. Once she came onboard, he gave it more energy. The upgraded showcase, *"Follow the Rainbow,"* became a popular event. The buzz attracted adult actresses and nomadic dancers, with loyal followings. Now, many of the men in attendance sat on millions. He introduced her to everyone, and advised her how to entice them.

JoJo handled the performers. He secured the venues, and hired the security, DJ, and host. They split the door and bar. He treated her as an equal. When she shared the news of Ish's party, he cheered. *"I want you to have everything your heart desires. I say, go for it!"*

He stopped in front of her house.

Where did the time go?

"That's some dank right there. Shit had me zoning the whole ride. My eyes were open, but I was all in my head."

"S'all good. I was vibin' too. I'll tell Dred, what you said. Hit me when you start moving around."

"For sure."

JoJo got out, and grumbled at the sky. Ready to erupt, pillows of dense clouds blocked the sun. She stood in the middle of the street and watched Rohan turn the corner.

Over an ear-splitting rumble, Mr. Rucks' shrill voice came out of thin air. "Caught that baw snooping around y'alls car this morning. I don't know what's come over him. He harasses Chanel when he thinks no one is looking. It ain't right."

"Thanks, Mr. Rucks."

"Seems to know how not to get caught. I may speak to his mama."

"I hope it doesn't come to that, but you're right about never catching him in the act."

"I used to have a good rapport with his grandmother. God rest her soul. Since she passed, he hasn't been the same. He doesn't work, and always smells like dope."

Although she had zero proof, JoJo's gut said, Biz shattered the house's back windows. She let it go when Chanel found someone to repair them within hours. In her opinion, she wasn't taking the hoodlum's threat serious enough, but she minded her business.

JoJo waved to Miss Richardson, who immediately spun in the opposite direction. The neighbor stopped acknowledging them altogether, a few months earlier. They assumed she was the person calling 9-1-1 anytime they lounged on the stoop past eleven p.m. Though strange, she was the meanest nor greediest person any of them had encountered while in town.

Lightning followed by a sharp, loud clap, sent her scurrying into the house. She called out, "Anyone home?" and waited.

Rain tapping against the window switched to rapid pitter-patter. When there was no response, she cut on the TV, and several lights to drown out the racket. Windows rattled. Toppled trashcans clanged.

The house went black and silent.

"Ugh!" She headed to the dining room, and fumbled in darkness until she found a candle and book of matches. Explosions of light, brightened the room. An indistinct noise captured her attention. She felt around for a weapon. With a vase in hand, she inched further towards the kitchen. Fear of nameless danger, made her question the wisdom of pressing forward. The glow from the pole in the alley, cast quivering shadows over the walls.

There's that sound again. The rain was now a full fledged downpour. The clatter of the windows was so loud, she wondered if they'd hold. Then she heard a louder thud, and knew she wasn't alone. Taking an intruder by surprise was her only chance of subduing them. She closed her eyes—*get to them, before they get to you!* The rumbling outside, masked the sound of her movement. As lightning flashed, she charged the archway.

"Holy crap!" Roxi was at the table with her head down. "Girl! You scared the shit out of me. Did you hear me ask if anyone was home? Why are you…" was all she got out before the lights in the living room and television, came back on. She flipped on the kitchen light, and noticed her puffy eye. She got closer to assess her injuries. "Who did this to you?"

"Country."

"What the fuck? For what? How long has he been beating you?"

She admitted, "It started a while ago," but that was only part of the story.

He stopped at the secluded park they visited when there wasn't time to go to a motel. The ride had been silent.

No—"*You look sexy*" or "*Lemme see what you can do with that mouth!*"

Always horny, his reserve should've set off alarms.

She climbed into the back of the Tahoe and got naked. He got in the back with her and unloosened his pants. Expecting him to whip out his dick, she licked her lips. He leaned back, and without warning, slapped his belt around her neck.

While struggling for oxygen, she felt his breath against her ear.

"*You're dead to me!*"

"*Why?*"

"*You're out here burning niggas. I should've known better than to fuck with a whore.*"

He'd given the girlfriend Roxi never knew existed an unspecified STD.

As her vision blurred, a sedan pulled up behind them. He unloosened the noose, slid it through the loops of his pants, and faced forward.

"*Lucky bitch!*"

She coughed and gagged, grateful for the interruption.

The trunk opened, and a family in helmets, began unloading bikes.

She knew he fucked other girls. "*How do you know, it was me?*"

The question riled him more. With the back of his hand, he slapped her again. "*Shut the fuck up. Ooh! You're so, so lucky!*"

He hopped behind the wheel and drove, hurling the most brutal insults she'd ever heard.

A mile from the house, he stopped. His lower lips quivered, as he reached into the back seat, gripped her by the collar and demanded she exit. "*If I ever see you again, I'ma stomp a mud hole in your ass and bury you where no one will find you!*"

JoJo banged her fist on the counter. "Roxi…come on. Are you serious? What have you been thinking?"

"It didn't start out this way. At first it was pinching. Then, he slapped me a few times, but always said sorry later. He isn't a bad person. We spent a lot of time together. I know all his friends and have met his kids. Shit, I know how he really makes his money. He does things to me, no man should do to a woman he doesn't love. I thought we had more."

"Pinching you. What kind of faggot shit is that? What am I here for?" She didn't want to hear anything about love. She'd sat in his chair, four times a month, for nearly year, and he never mentioned a disagreement. JoJo felt hurt, and foolish.

Roxi unloosened her robe, wincing with every flex. Fresh bruises covered her arms, but the faded marks shined, like glowing coals. "I knew we still owed him for the car. He kept pressing me. He was relentless. I kept seeing him, hoping he'd let it go."

"Girl!—Forget him, and that piece of crap car. I swear you've got a heart of gold, but do some of the dumbest shit. I thought you hooked up with him because you liked him."

"I did, at first."

"Don't worry about that car. He can have the motherfucker back. It stays in the damn shop anyway." The phone in the living room rang. "Wait a minute."

"Yeah!"

"Yeah? Is that how you answer the phone?"

"No—you're right." She softenined her tone. "My bad. Whats up? Did I leave something?"

"Nah. Is everything okay? You sound stressed."

"I'll be fine. Just got some shocking news. Niggas ain't shit."

"Sorry to hear. Want to talk about it?"

"Not really."

"Good."

"What's up with you?"

"Ain't shit."

"You should be home by now."

"I realized we haven't talked in a minute, so I circled back. I'm glad I called. You up for riding out for a few."

"Sure. Got something on your mind?"

"Nothing major. You hungry? We can discuss the party. The big day is coming up."

"That would be cool. Thank you. How long before you get here?"

"*I'm* at your door."

Her heart cheered. "Cool. Gimme a sec."

"Take your time."

JoJo returned to the kitchen, and found Roxi hadn't budged. She wanted to thrash her for looking so pitiful. "I'll never understand you letting some nigga put his hands on you and not tell anyone."

"It makes no sense when you say it like that. I messed up. I thought I could hold my own, but percs, *maaan*—they are something entirely different. You didn't know it, but I been caught up for a minute. I need help, but it doesn't excuse what he did to me."

"You're right about that. He'll get his. Give me some time to think about this. Fuck that punk. Real men don't hit women."

"Why does shit like this keep happening? Do you think I'm cursed?"

Before responding, she gave the questions some thought. *To keep doing the same thing, expecting a different result is textbook insanity, but Roxi is far from crazy.*

"I don't think your cursed. You need to stop looking for love in all the wrong places. A good friend told me—the devil has a plot, but God has a plan. I believe there's someone specially made by God for all of us. You just got to pick them better."

Roxi inhaled deeply. "Thanks for always having my back."

"No doubt."

JoJo was near the door when she stopped.

"Rox—you ever thought about rehab?"

"Some."

"Maybe, it would help."

30

THE BBC

"*Put the word out. A few heads will come through.*"
When Ish boasted, he was being modest. Within hours of passing out the first flyer, JoJo's phone was on fire. The "*Birthday Bash*" was the most anticipated event in years. In addition to being a High School hoop star, his best friend was head of a Westside mob. With deep citywide ties, the fifty-dollar advance tickets, sold briskly.

Hood royalty dallied with *degulars*, and the *unaffiliated* on rare occasions, but when they did, anything could pop off. Social climbers put on their best, and tried their damnedest to be noticed. One conversation, could alter a guy or girl's existence.

During the weeks leading up to the party, the girls hit up every lounge, go-go bar, barber shop, check cashing place, hair salon, and hole in the wall, on the East and Westside. For the first time, they touched all parts of the city—*Park Heights, Reisterstown Road, Liberty Heights, Garrison, Walkbrook Junction, Poplar Grove, Pennsylvannia Ave, North Ave, Cloverdale, Whitelock, Westside Shopping Center, Edmonson Village, Pulaski Street, Clay Street, Oldtown Mall, Monument Street, Up the Hill, Down the Hill, Preston Street, Greenmount Ave, The Dome, Belair Road, Four by Four, Erdman Ave, Wilkens Ave, Brooklyn, Annapolis Road, Cherry Hill, Patapsco Flea Market*, and numerous other enclaves, they impulsively tripped into.

Their efforts paid off, as partygoers from both halves of the city, converged on the small strip club. Initally, she feared it would be a sausage party, but sexy women came out in droves.

They club owner shimmied up to her, estatic the line stretched around the block. He'd spent millions renovating the former burlesque parlor, and hoped this event put his *"baby"* on the map. "Are you ready to rock and roll?"

"Yessir, lets do this!"

She nervously watched the first thirty patrons enter. She'd taken Rohan's advice, regarding the price of admission. A few redeemed tickets, but most were stepping to the cashier. The seventy-five dollar admission price wasn't a deterrant.

Cha-ching!

Ishmael's arrival caused a commotion. JoJo relieved the panicky helper before things got out of hand. "The twenty odd people bum rushing security, aren't on the guest list. I didn't want to let them in for free because I'd have to deal with you."

"You did right. I got it from here."

"Can you tell those guys its cool? The little blue-black one scares me."

"I will. You're doing fine. Don't let this get to you."

"Thanks."

Ish struggled to quiet his crew. She tapped his shoulder. "What's up, birthday boy! Can I help?"

"What up! *Man*—its looking nice up in here. Glad to know people got love for the kid."

"Hell yeah. It's already exceeded my expectations. We went hard. Told everybody we knew, who'd tell everyone they knew, and bam!"

"Thanks, again."

"No problem."

"Sorry bout that shit at the door. I'll holla at them lil niggas. Apologize to your doormen for my man grabbing him. Shit wasn't called for. They'll be no more static. I promise. We're here to have a good time."

"Don't think any more about it. Push it all out your mind.

How many people are with you?"

"I should have told you in advance, but I got 9 niggas with me. Whats the cover?"

"Don't worry. Let's go get them. Point em out." He led the way.

Minutes later, several dancers appeared, and led the men through the club. Ish shook hands with attendees. His companions waved. Stanchion posts and velour ropes marked the area, reserved for the VIP contingent. Gold-wrapped bottles, large bowls of ice, carafes of juice, and a humidor of Chobibas, sat on a long table. When they were seated, DJ DNA announced, "Yo-Yo-Yo! The BBC is in the building!"

JoJo let them settle in before reapproaching. Ish addressed the four men at his table—"Listen up. This is my homegirl, JoJo. She's from ova East, but…. she put this whole thing together." All of them laughed at his jibe, except for one of them.

"I'm from ova East, now? How y'all doing? What chu sippin?"

"Hen dog—, Heneiken—, Crown and Coke—, Jack—, Water."

"Okay. I'll make sure you're taken care of. What about you, super star? If you not feeling what's here already, I can get you something else."

"Nah—I'ma fuck with that Cris. I want you to meet my best friend."

"Cool."

"Sci!" One of his tablemates leaned forward.

It would be the dude with the stink face.

She answered his ambiguous scowl with a smile.

"*Eh* Yo, this is the one I told you about."

"Wassup."

"Nice to meet you. This turn out is really something."

"I spy a lot of thirstbuckets, and niggas I've been ducking, but other than that—bravo."

Ish threw his head back, and looked at the ceiling. "Come on, yo."

"Aiight. It's your day."

"You're right about that! JoJo, I think I'll take you up on that offer of something else to drink. Bring me, and my man double Jacks."

Science held up his bottle and shook it. "Nah—I'm good."

She'd never met anyone that sucked the moisture out of the air. With eyes cast to the ground, as people swirled merrily around, his agitation, and discomfort were apparent.

That's one strange dude!

"I got you. I'll be right back."

While walking away, she heard Ish snap. "All this ass in one room, and you're uptight. My nigga, breathe—relax."

She'd heard about Science, the Westside D-boy, with tentacles stretching throughout the city. All the girls thought he was cute, but wished he didn't look so mean. She agreed he was handsome, but also knew he battled demons. *Sympathies for anyone who crosses or decieves him.*

With his drink in hand, JoJo pulled Ish to the side. Something inside of her needed confirmation she hadn't offended his guy. "Why doesn't your homeboy like me?"

He sighed. This wasn't the first time he'd explained his best friend's demeanor. "Don't take it personal. That's how that nigga is. This ain't his scene. He's only here on the strength of me. I'm grateful."

"Yeah well—I don't know what you told him about me."

"You're trippin'. I ain't told him nothing. What's there to say? You're good people."

"Aiight. If you say so. Baltimore niggas wild with that mean muggin'. Ion know what to make of it."

"Well, look at you. He's probably scared you want to square up with him."

"You're crazy. I'm a lover, not a fighter."

"I hear you, Miss Lover."

"Are you planning to walk around?"

"I think, I'll hang out here. The set up's dope. You should get our girl to come over, and keep me company."

She'd booked well-known performers from other cities, but

he wanted Nella's recognition. "I can do that. Let me find her. Give me a minute." Her eyes were fixed on a group of guys entering the club. She'd been waiting on one of them all night.

"No rush. For now..." Ish looked at his friends. "I'ma see what's up with the shorty in red."

JoJo raised her chin, and grinned. "I ain't never had chicks fight over who could work an event until this shit right here. The one you're checking for, got it bad for you. Watch out, now!"

They both laughed, as Ish slid away. She overheard him say, before sharing a group embrace. "Who loves you, baby?"

Ish tried to quell her angst, but Science scared her. As if he heard her thoughts, their eyes met. She lowered her gaze.

After mingling and taking pictures with people she didn't know, JoJo spent the remainder of the night in a dark corner. As she watched the comings and goings, it felt awesome seeing her vision come to life.

Ego aside, there was so much shit on her plate. Nella fucked one of Roxi's regulars—major *"hoe code"* violation. Sleeping with each other's clients was a *"No, No,"* but men loved hopping beds. Makes you wonder why some are pissed or forlorn, when it happens.

The two came the closest to blows she'd ever seen them. Only Chanel had the adeptness to calm them down. She sparked three joints of blueberry, and made them see fighting each other wasn't worth it. By the time they were high, they were giggling, and talking about outshining the other. Though things quieted down, the dust up made parting ways inevitable.

"Look at you, shawd! This turnout is aiight! I should've put you in charge of promoting our shit!"

She turned around. Rohan grabbed her by the shoulders, and smiled. "I'm not counting your cheese, but I know you caked."

"It feels good."

"Looks like you don't need me anymore."

"You're crazy. I'd never break up the band. In this case though—it was all Ish. People fucks with him."

"Yeah—I hear you. That's my man. This is a come up none

the less."

"I agree."

"We're gonna get up out of here. I've gotta drop a few niggas off, then take this ride."

"I feel you on that. Thanks again for coming out."

"*Whaad!* I wouldn't have missed it, but I already ran into my wife's girlfriend, and I'm not trying to hear her mouth."

She felt a twinge of envy, but wished him well. "Drive safe."

The vibe remained upbeat as the festivities weened. Ish got his "*quality time*" with Nella. The two stayed glued for the final hour, sneaking kisses, when they thought no one was looking.

Impossible! Eyes were glued on their display.

To the dismay of those who knew Ish's generous reputation, he and his boys, never made it rain. They had to be content with the *dum dums*, tossing ones for fun, over substance, or a connection with a real kingpin.

When the party ended, JoJo proudly handed him six grand. The majority of it came from the presales.

"Word? Yo—that's love!" Shocked by her largesse, he put the money in his pocket and checked for watchers. "This was one of the best birthdays ever. I appreciate all you did to make that happen."

He didn't know it, but this had been the most rewarding experience of her life. With the bar, and picture man split, and the almost seven grand they rang at the door, she was ending the night with a little over ten stacks.

Science tapped Ish on the shoulder. "You ready?"

"Hell yeah. Holla at me tomorrow, shawd."

"For sure. Nice to meet you."

Science jiggled his keys.

"Have you seen my baby?"

"She's by the front door. That's you, tonight?"

"Yeah man—she's the truth."

JoJo grinned. "I've heard."

31

TRICKERIES

"**R**o, you're not gonna believe this one." JoJo didn't believe, what she'd heard, herself. "You got a minute?"

"For you—sure." The yelping puppies in the background made it hard to hear. "I'm feeding Midnight and Winter. Hold on."

"Do you."

He and a brother ran a kennel out of their mother's back yard. Their money-makers were pits, but they'd begun experimenting with Mastiffs. The brutes ate more raw meat each day than a family in a week, but he was all in.

She hated disturbing him. It was the busiest part of his day, but they hadn't talked since the party, which by all accounts, had been a success. *The big shots came out, nobody got shot, and the birthday boy left with a bag!*

She hadn't even celebrated her "win" before getting bad news.

A few minutes later, he returned to the phone. "You still there?"

"Of course."

"Good. Talk to me. Wassup?"

"The morning after the party, Ish and Nella got robbed coming out of their room."

"What? I don't believe it."

"Yup—hmmmph!"

"How is that possible? What they get off em?"

"She didn't get into specifics."

"What hotel?"

"The Executive Suites on Orleans."

"Niggas stay in that mah-fuggah?"

"You're funny. I think they recently renovated it."

"Damn. Go head, keep talking."

They both laughed.

"I don't have all the facts, but I know they had ski masks and guns. I'm still putting together the pieces, and I hate to say it but, Snow White's story isn't adding up. She also waited a whole day to tell me."

JoJo couldn't wait to see Ish and get his side, but he wasn't answering the phone. *What the fuck is really going on?* If the situation felt suspect to her, Science felt it too.

I don't want to be on his radar.

"I'll say it, since you won't—shit sound like some flim flam."

"I'm glad to hear you feel it too."

"Who takes a nigga off when he leaving the room with his girl? Seems like a lot of risk, when you're not even sure, how much money's there?"

"Right!" *If this bitch is responsible, I'll tell them where to find her.*

Rohan hadn't brought up Nella's character in the past because he hated gossip, but this was the second tale he'd heard involving her and masked robbers. He planned to do some digging, and wanted JoJo to start covering her ass, until he got back to her. "Damn—well, there's not much you can do right now, other than holler at that man. You need to get to the bottom of this, before things get out of hand."

"I've been hitting him, since I heard the news." The last thing she wanted, was for Ish to think she was involved in any way, shape, or form.

"I'm sure it's all good. Don't stress. What else is new?"

"Not much. Still in chill mode for real."

"You did your thing with the party. Cars were still pulling up when I rolled out. The streets are still talking."

"Yeah, man. It turned out pretty nice. Looks like you were right. I stressed myself out for nothing."

"I tried to tell you."

"Will I see you later?"

"Not tonight. You know what I gotta do in the a.m. I'm chillin. Mom's cooking five cheese mac, mustards, and baked turkey wings. The first kick off is at one, then another, at eight."

"Oh, right. How could I forget? Enjoy yourself. I'll let you know what I find out."

"You do that. Need be—we can tie Nella ass up, and *yaaah mean*, til she come clean."

"I don't know bout all that, but I may need to cut the bitch off."

"It's your call, but say the word, and I got you."

"Be safe. Love you."

"You too, shordy. I'll holla at ya tomorrow."

JoJo walked into the living room with a smile on her face. The Camry keys on the mantle, darkened her mood. Country still needed to be taught a lesson, but she didn't have any good options. He was Biz's friend, and Gus was weak. Rohan had her back, but that was using a chainsaw to do surgery. Besides, she hated when chicks got men involved in domestic disturbances. The house phone rang. *"Woooo-saaah!"*

"Hello."

"Whaaaazzup!"

"Who's this?"

"Whaaaazzup!"

"Stop playing!"

"Just fuckin' with you, shawd. It's your number one fan."

"I'm gonna hang up."

"It's Ish. Damn, you're tough."

"Nah—what's good? I've been tryna holla at you. Can we meet up?"

"Sure thing. Meet me at Rodeo's in forty minutes."

"Bet. See you soon."

32

CLEARING THE AIR

"**Y**ou're dead wrong, and you know it! Picking up a fare when the back of your ride smells like a damn barn. Pee Yew!"

Without turning around, the cabbie shouted, "My name is not Pee Yew! It's Serge'. And I advise you to shut up or get out! You confused soul. Sounding like a woman, but looka like a man!"

JoJo laughed. *Sir-gay mad!* Immigrants, always resorted to dissing her appearance. "Try being original!"

He turned up the radio's volume, and mumbled something indecipherable. Now, on top of the funk, frenetic eighties synth pop tunes, assaulted her other senses. Rather than fight, she opened the window, and breathed out of her mouth.

After a month-long hiatus, they'd soon be back on the road. Rohan's homeboy was taking them to the auction. He had a dealer's license, and claimed Camrys, similar to the one they bought, sold daily for four to five hundred dollars. *Country's ass, probably paid a similar price!*

When they arrived at her destination, Serge' never turned around. Instead, he pointed to the meter on the dash —"$9.40." As she decamped, she crumbled a ten dollar bill, and aimed it at the back of his head. The angry man sped off, screaming something in another language.

She couldn't miss Ish in the front row with a dancer—*up close and personal*. She hesitated to interrupt their moment.

He slid a twenty in her garter, copping a feel of her ample bottom. She flipped over, and jiggled her cheeks before slowly crawling away.

JoJo sat next to him.

"Hey. When did you come in?"

"A second a go, but you were busy."

"Not really."

"Where've you been?"

"Maaan! I bit the bullet, and hopped on a red eye—west. Spent a week out in Vegas, won a lil something, then headed out to LA, for a few days. I know a few folks out there, doing it big. I'm just getting back."

"Good to see you. Sounds like you had a blast."

"Yeah, I needed it."

"If you don't mind, I'd like to get to the main reason I'm here."

"Go for it."

"I heard about you and Nella. That had to have been unreal. What happen?"

"Science dropped us off at the mote."

"I'm down."

"You know—we've gone there before. It's close to the city. Clean. Low key. Anyway—we stepped out the room, and were mid-way down the steps, when they ran at us, from both directions. One nigga was at the top, and another was coming from the bottom towards us. I'd given Nella two grand of what you gave me, and I had a couple hundred in my sock. I also had the five grand, Science gave me for my birthday in my backpack. I wish I would've asked him to hold it, when he dropped us off. Those niggas took everything from both of us. I ain't worried bout that shit though. Money comes, money goes. Nella's okay. Fuck it. It's only bread. I make it every day."

Interesting. Though he didn't find the circumstances of the robbery odd her *Spidey* senses were tingling.

Miss Nella Blanco left some details out of her account.

Did she think I wouldn't confirm the story, or that Ish wouldn't tell me about the money?

"Wassup with Nella? She acted like she was so busy tonight."

"Ish, I don't know how to say this any other way so I'm gonna be blunt. Some women like being free to come and go as they please. Nella is one of them. You will never be more than what you already are, believe me." JoJo knew her comment stung, but better she tell him, than for Nella to fuck it up for everyone. "You know the saying about tryna turn a hoe into a housewife. It's true. Don't complicate something simple."

"I hear you."

"No—I don't think you do. You're a stand up dude, and your heart seems to be in the right place. Find a girl that can appreciate you. Nella will consume you. She's a man eater— pretty, but emotionally unavailable."

Ish was disappointed, but didn't let it show. No matter what JoJo said, for him, he believed their connection could grow. She'd told him about her desire for children, and interest in photojournalism. They'd spent many nights together, some without sex, and money was never an issue. She had bills to pay so he always left something on the table. He also knew looking good got expensive.

"I appreciate you tryna look out for me."

"I try. Thanks. So, what's the plan for the rest of the evening? Can't have you looking like you lost your puppy."

"Nah. I'm straight. I'ma get us a shot, then we're gonna tip some skeezers."

"By the way, my home girl KD from DC. Hold up—that rhymed." She smiled. "As I was saying—my friend is gonna meet us here. I hope you don't mind. She's never been to Baltimore. I wanna show her a good time."

"That's what's up. I'd love to hang out with y'all."

They ordered drinks, and an *old hand* with red hair appeared, asking if he wanted a dance. Ish seemed to like her, so she didn't knock auntie's hustle.

Her peace was interrupted by a bump to her chair. She twisted around to find a pretty face with an attitude. "Well if it isn't Miss Kitty. Hot pink is a good color on you. You look nice, tonight."

"Whatever. Don't come at me like that. I look good every night."

Kitty has to be the saltiest bitch alive! She was a six in terms of looks, but her mouth was reportedly "a ten." In some respects, JoJo owed her, for her spot, in the game. For green, she'd swallow her pride, if it got Kitty on the team.

"The disrespect is unnecessary. I only said, you look nice. Let's start over. I get it—you're upset, but you're looking at this wrong. There's enough meat on the bone for all of us—if you'd act like a lady."

"I'll tell you like I told that bitch Nella, get in my fucking way, and I'll kick your asses back to the swamp. It would seem y'all don't understand the pecking order round here. This is my city. Fuck what bloated ass Rohan told you. Ya boy's gonna get his. None of y'all gawn mess up my money."

Ro was fam, but it wasn't necessary she understand. Backing down wasn't her style, but quarrelling over some *he said, she said* shit, was stupid. The girls had more business than they could handle.

Let me simplify shit for this idiot! "We ain't going nowhere. You can dislike me, but you're not stopping my grind. From where I sit, you got two choices—kick rocks, or we link up like Super Friends, and take over. More entertainers in the mix equals fewer customers turned away."

Kitty stepped back, sucked her teeth, and stared at JoJo like she'd grown a second head. "No thanks. You're an amateur, who'll never be in my league. I heard about the party you threw for the West side nigga. I'll give you credit for pulling that off, but you ain't slick."

"Okay...cool. I'll take that."

"You ain't running a damn thang. And keep your views on me, to yourself. I am 100% lady. What are you?"

JoJo suppressed an urge to laugh. "What?" She couldn't believe Kitty's bombastic reaction. "Relax. No need to raise your voice. I don't wanna beef. I come offering solutions, and you wanna get smart."

"Solutions? For who? You're sneaky, and you roll with the snakiest of snakes." She then addressed Ish. "You better watch this bitch."

"Bitch?" *Hmmm.* Well, Kitty—it was nice chatting with you."

"Stay out of my way!"

Ish smiled, amused by the interchange.

Before storming off, she fumed. "I'll see you."

JoJo threw up a peace sign then slammed her fist on the counter. "You hear that nonsense?"

"Running her mouth. Talking bout people, and don't even know who's sitting in her face.

"Right! Baltimore chicks got to be some of the dumbest on this planet. I swear—nobody graduates from High School, or thinks things through."

"Some, not all."

"I haven't met a bright one, yet."

"You're crazy." Ish sipped his drink. "I can't lie—that was bugged out. I wanted to see what else she'd say. You be going through it, I see."

"Me? Not really. I stay in the cut, as you B'More folk say."

"I hear that, but you can't fool me. I heard about you putting paws on a few bitches."

"Every one of those situations, involved someone thinking, me or my girls were lames."

"Her damn head was twirling so much, I thought it might pop off—literally."

"I'm not paying her no mind. I hate getting angry. It's not me. That girl don't want it with me, for real. You heard me propose a way for 'us' to win."

"You on some family shit. That ain't for everyone."

"She lacks creativity when it comes to getting money and blames me. It ain't my fault."

"They call that cutting off your nose to spite your face."

"That's a good ass way to put it."

JoJo was happy to know, at least in his mind, the robbery was a random occurrence. Ish's version of the event made Nella a liar. *She has to go!*

Ro's insight, was critical for planning her follow-up. She couldn't wait to share what she'd learned.

Ish giving Nella his cut from the party, pissed her off. It felt like food had been snatched from her mouth.

33

ROHAN

*R*ohan stepped out the front door, bright eyed, and ready to tackle the day. Concealed by the trees, alert starlings belted staccato songs. A fresh round of snow fell overnight. Happy he'd worn a thicker coat, he scanned the street for signs of life, before tackling the slick stairs.

The Q45's windows were completely fogged when he started the car. Clouds formed in front of him with each exhale. He turned his collar up, and rubbed his hands in front of the center vents.

The radio was on 92Q from the night before. A reporter read the headlines—*"Three people killed over night; two of them were teens. A water line break on Greene Street, and a fire in the northbound Ft. McHenry tunnel; expect delays."*

Same *ole same ole* crossed his mind as he flipped through the stations. He paused as a song his mother loved came on.

Can't go wrong with Heaven 600.

Getting up early and going out into the cold were neck and neck for his least favorite things to do. Few could get him to budge when he didn't want to, but he'd do anything for *"Ma Dukes."* Three times a week, for two hours in the morning, dialysis was their routine.

Afterwards, when she didn't feel weak, they drove to the Cherry Hill Rowing Club, and fed the ducks. She didn't grow up in Baltimore. The setting reminded her of *"home."* On benches

185

overlooking the water, they held hands, laughed, and made up for lost time. He especially loved her stories, interwoven with rebel wisdom. Most he'd heard, but he now appreciated more.

He regretted his years of reckless behavior, and estrangement from his family. At thirty, and a married father of three, he better understood the type of man she'd raised him to be. Of all the children, he'd caused the most, grey hairs. As a consequence, he was honored to step up in this small, but necessary way. As long as there was breath in his body, he'd care for her, and never complain. He owed her a debt of gratitude, he'd never fully repay.

The windows were clear. The interior was toasty. He looked to his right. His mother stood in the doorway, outfitted for a blizzard, and smiling.

After unlocking the door, he checked the side view mirror for traffic. A kid dressed in black, including his mask, rode alongside the car on a bike. Rohan watched him pull the *Nano* from his dip, but couldn't stop him, from dropping, and peddling off.

34

GUT PUNCH

"Ro...Ro—Han...**sniff sniff** this morning...**sniff sniff** Rohan is dead."

"What?" JoJo prayed she hadn't heard the distraught caller correctly.

"Ye—yeah. They killed him, yo."

"Nooooo! Come on. Why?" she screamed, bowing to a wave of sorrow. She and Scooter bawled like babes. Soon as one stopped, the other stirred him or her, to start again.

"Jo—Jo, I'm stuck," he told her between sniffles. "They killed my best... best friend. What am I going to do?"

"Where did this happen? I spoke with him, late last night."

"He was warming up the car, and a nigga ran up on him. Worse part about it—my mama seen all of it. She's in Mercy now. She tumbled over the oxygen tank cord. She fell...**sniff sniff** down the steps, and fractured her jaw. My whole family's fucked up. I'm waiting on a train to Baltimore, now. If you pray, please, say one for us."

"I will. If there is anything you need...anything I can do, I'm here for you."

He composed himself before continuing. "You and big bro were tight...so I thought it was only right...I call, and tell you. I'll holla at you."

"Thanks for calling. Scooter—I'm sure you know, but your brother loved you so much."

"No problem. And, I know. Rohan told me every day. I'll talk to you soon."

"Okay."

Despite the early hour, JoJo bought a fifth of Remy Martin 1738. It wasn't XO, his favorite, but the substitute would do in a pinch. She took a sip before leaving the store.

Back home, with zero reasons to remain cognizant, she guzzled the numbing agent. She fell apart, thinking of never talking to her mentor, and dream lover again.

Separate and aside from Rohan's death, she also worried about how they'd cover the month's bills. They had shut off notices for both the water and electricity. The cable had been out since the beginning of the week, but no one seemed to notice. The last thing she planned to do was come out of pocket *again* for grown women.

As she considered the disregard for their agreement, she became angrier. Unlike a pimp, she didn't extort, physically abuse, or play with the girls' minds. Two hundred dollars a week should have been nothing. Instead, they fed her meandering stories about geriatric pervs and fuckboys.

Not my problem!

Taking advantage of my generosity, ends today!

They'll sit in the dark if that's what it takes for them to understand—I'm done.

She wanted to give up the reigns.

I'm tired of this life!

I got all these bitches with me, yet I feel all alone.

But, do what?

Admit defeat, and go back to Merle? Go back home?

Hell no! I'd rather sell drugs.

With a cloudy mind and heavy heart, she ran to her room, and locked the door. After putting on an R&B mixtape, she got under the covers, and began snoring.

That evening, Nella, who'd been M.I.A. for days, arrived and told the girls about the slaying. Each liked Rohan, but knew he and JoJo were close. "Let's make sure she's okay."

All three stood in the hallway as Chanel knocked, and offered words of encouragement. After five minutes of non-response, the trio headed down stairs, single file. Sensing tension from both, Nella grabbed her purse, and split without saying goodbye.

"Eh Rox, you tryna hang out with my people from up top tonight?"

"Who?"

"Remember the guy Brody I told you I was dating? He's the one who gave me fifteen hundred dollars shaped like a bouquet of roses, and bought me the LV wallet you uncovered being nosey. Remember the pictures I showed you, with me and the Dominican papi, in the big ass babushka hats."

She laughed. "Yeah—I think I remember."

"You know who I'm talking about."

"I don't know. Maybe."

"His main man, Prince, is gonna be with him. You know he's fine if I'm vouching. Pockets stay poppin. Gucci down to the socks. Drives a Maserati."

For the prior six months she'd been kicking it with the slickster from Harlem—two weekends a month, and he spoiled her rotten. The *"Biz debacle"* forced her to stop messing with *"locals,"* altogether. *"They're needy, don't have enough money, and most of them are borderline retarded. I bet it's all the lead in the water!"*

Loving him was easy. He treated her like a queen. The last three trips, he gave her a G for every brick she bought back on the train. With more money, than she'd ever had at one time, she felt fortunate. They discussed her moving up, but for the time being, agreed to let their relationship evolve naturally.

Tonight, she'd wine, and dine him.

Dinner, then a Hyatt suite, overlooking Harborplace—

It's gonna be awesome!

Roxi was sure the guy was cute, with money to burn, but

she'd planned to turn in early. Her body still ached. A bath and a blunt were calling her name. Plus, she hated being the only one who didn't speak *Español*. "I kinda want to chill. I didn't know Rohan well, but I've smoked with the nigga. It's kinda messed up I won't be able to do that again."

"The Big Black situation is bugged, but you can do 'nothing,' tomorrow? The least we can do is make some money to help out, until she figures out our next move."

"There's money involved?"

"Maybe. I know he'll like you."

"You're right…Okay. I'll go with you."

"You won't regret it. Make sure you thank a bitch later."

Roxi sucked her teeth, and playfully rolled her eyes. "What are you wearing?"

"It's cold as a white man out there…so definitely a sweater. Maybe the cream cowl neck with some light wash jeans, and platform booties. My boo likes the way stilettos make my choo-choo stick out."

"I heard that. Dat caboose is phat. You can wear my fox if you want. It would match perfectly."

"*Ohhh*—that's an idea. Let me get back to you on that." Chanel laughed at her new angle. *This little girl will never learn? You cannot borrow my clothes!* "Let's sit for a minute. I swear, I hate winter."

"Speaking of cold, you see how Nella skated out of here?"

"She better had. You know—a little birdie told me, she sets niggas up."

"Yeah well—I'm not surprised at all. Make sure your ducks are in a row when you take it to JoJo. That's her girl."

Roxi nodded in agreement. "Oh, I will! How they say it in B'more—best believe!"

35

IF IT'S NOT ONE THING, IT'S ANOTHER

*T*he foursome arrived at *Dockside's*, and selected seats along the large mahogany bar. Knicks versus Golden State blazed across a big screen. The neighboring ten-top was unappealing, but the heated playoff season intrigued them. They put their apprehension aside, and debated the enormous menu. After smashing two platters of oysters, they ordered steamed shrimp, lamp lollipops, crab balls, and shots of tequila.

Words dripped from Prince's lips like honey off the comb. His gear and shape up were fresh, but—so what. She loved compliments, but they didn't pay the bills. Her mother always said, *"A dry purse and wet ass don't mix!"* Unmoved by his artful seduction, she hoped his tongue game was on point. She had a feeling he wasn't packing.

"You like boy?"

"Boy, boy?"

"White boy."

"I, dib and dab. Why do you ask?"

"No real reason. I'm just tryna see how you roll. Our friends are wrapped up in their own conversation, and seeing as though we're kicking it tonight, I'd like us to get comfortable." He leaned closer, and put his hand on her leg.

"You got some?"

"Go in the bathroom with me. They won't even notice we're gone."

"Are you serious?"

"Come on—live a little."

"We'll be right back." Roxi and Prince locked arms, and disappeared.

Chanel and Brody barely noticed the departure. So captivated by the verbal image he painted, she missed Kitty joining the party behind them.

The daring duo waited for a lady to exit, then slipped into the woman's restroom. Prince kicked open a door, and allowed Roxi to enter first. He pulled a square of newspaper from his Pelle Pelle, unfolded it, and let her inspect it.

Her spine tingled. "Looks good."

He warned. "Take your time. I recognize the look. This ain't that brown shit."

"I see."

She rolled a dollar bill, dipped the quill into the powder, and inhaled. Prince took one of his own, pinched his nose, and closed his eyes. For the minutes that followed, both stood paralyzed, as the sedative took effect.

Through the euphoria, they heard loud voices and shrieks, followed by someone crashing through the entrance. Banging on the first stall, snapped Prince out of his nod.

"Yo, kid—let's get up out of here!" Brody roared, hammering his fist into his open palm, for emphasis. "*Yooooo!* Chop chop, my nigga. Eh Roxi, tell baby girl to call me."

Prince adjusted his clothes, and wiped the residual residue from his nose. "What's good?"

"Come awn, son. Time to break out!" He paced back and forth, while shouting. "B'more crazier than a muthafucka, yo! We gotta go!"

He kissed Roxi on the forehead. "I'll holla at you when I'm in these parts again."

She washed her hands, and splashed water on her cheeks. She grabbed a stack of napkins, then went to find Chanel.

She found her on the floor with a crowd standing above her

screaming for help. Blood from a facial gash, leaked through her fingers. Roxi folded the paper towels in half, and pressed it against the wound. They soaked through in less than a minute. Others brought more, but the fluid kept seeping.

"Someone…anyone please call 9-1-1."

A patron near the front door screamed, "Sista—we called. They're on the way!"

Chanel whispered "*Kit*," before losing consciousness.

When the paramedics arrived, Roxi rang the house hoping JoJo was awake. After calling several times, back to back, she finally answered. "Thank you, Jesus! It's Roxi. Chanel's been hurt. They're loading her into the ambo."

"What?"

"Oh—JoJo. I fucked up. I'm so dumb. I should've never left her alone."

"Slowdown. You're not making sense."

"Kitty. She cut her. Oh, Jesus—there's so much blood."

"I just talked to that bitch. Where are you?"

"At Dockside's."

"Doing what?"

"We were here with friends."

"Where were you when this happened? Did you sit there and watch?"

"No. It didn't happen like that. I was in the bathroom. What did you say to her? Why would she take things so far?"

"I don't know, but I'ma find out. Where is she now?"

"Who? Kitty? They're gone."

"No, Roxi! Chanel—where is she?"

"They're strapping her to the gurney, as we speak."

"Where are they taking her?"

Roxi groaned. "I don't know."

"Go ask!"

The receiver dangled while she questioned the EMT. She returned, seconds later. "Hopkins!"

"I'll see you there!" JoJo threw the phone against the wall.

36

THE BAG

Seated at the kitchen table, JoJo listened to the last *"drip... drip...drip"* of the brewing process. The eleven minutes it took to brew a pot of coffee, had never felt so long. She was exhausted, and hoped to stop yawning.

After preparing a large cup, she sat down to rest her curiously sore knee. Details of the prior night were sketchy.

Of all the days for something to pop off!

Seeing Chanel, bloodied and suffering, filled her with rage. She wished she'd been more in control of her emotions, but she was in pain. Rohan's murder hurt worse, than any loss, she'd ever endured. Life no longer made sense. The pressure of being *"responsible,"* weighed on her.

After hours of watching *"white coats"* pass, she demanded, *"Service!"* Her subsequent directives were utterly disrespectful.

Post-ejection, she walked home, nursing the remaining Remy.

From the distance, she noticed someone sitting on her steps.

"Gus?" she recalled asking with hesitation. *"What do you want?"*

He hadn't been in her bed in over a month. She would've bet her last dollar, he'd been in jail, or under Tashia's thumb.

His weak chin pissed her off.

"I heard about what happened to your main man. I came to check on you."

"You're an asshole."

Unable to think, she begged. *"Please, help me into the house."*

He assisted her to the couch, and took off her shoes.

"What's your angle?" She remembered asking. *"Sympathy dick?"*

"It's nothing like that. I care about you."

She laid long ways, and closed her eyes. *"You're wack!"*

The world around her faded to black.

She woke up in the same place. Gus was gone. After a shower, she realized Nella's possessions, and her checkbook, were missing too.

JoJo tore up her room, but knew where she'd left it. She kept all of her important documents in one place—*third drawer, under the jeans, in a manila envelope.*

Gus' phone kept going to voice mail, and she couldn't rule out any of the girls.

She'd locked her door the night before, but found it open. The thief was even nice enough to leave the key on the kitchen table.

The thought of somebody going through her drawers, made her blood boil. Her only solace—*the bank is closed.*

Roxi walked into the kitchen yawning. *"Morning."* In her hand were the sunglasses and Dior Saddle bag, she'd lifted from Nella's closet, the prior day.

"Where'd you find that?"

"I tried telling you—that sheisty bitch was up to no good."

One Mogadishu...Two Mogadishu...Three Mogadishu...Four... JoJo hated people, snooping through other people's stuff.

"I did it to prove a point."

"Your intention is insignificant. Regardless of how you feel right now, do you like people going through your shit?"

"No."

"Well, don't do it to other people."

"Your girl's got a lot..."

JoJo raised her hand. "Please stop. Not, my girl."

"She ain't right. That hoe needs to go."

"Honestly, I've got bigger problems. I don't care about no ugly pocketbook."

"Since she been with us she's done nothing, but feed herself."

Same as everyone else!

"I blame myself for bringing her into our midst. I'll fix it."

"I hope so."

JoJo rubbed her three-inch bush and admitted, *a good barber was impossible to find.* Country's gift with clippers couldn't be denied. The last guy she tried, pushed her hairline back on the sides. Luckily, it grew back without permanent effect, but she felt rugged as shit. Thinking about it incensed her further. "Enough about that! What happened yesterday? Where were you when Chanel got jumped?"

After an extended pause, "I'm gonna be honest. I was in the bathroom sniffing blow with Prince."

"What?" She hadn't expected the response. While she appreciated bluntness, *"sniffing blow"* felt graphic. "I thought you quit the hard stuff after you stop seeing Country."

She joined JoJo at the table. "I can't lie—E's had me slippin', but I've chilled since then. I've never shot up and never will. Boy isn't my thing, but I said fuck it. We were heading to the hotel, a little later. I wanted to loosen up. I didn't wanna go in the first place, but Chanel reminded me about—you know, the house. I got pretty, and put on a happy face. He was cute, and we were vibin', but something was missing. When he whipped it out, all I could think about was getting where I needed to be, to do what needed to be done."

Roxi never ceased amazing her.

Treatment clearly isn't on her mind. I'll never bring it up again.

"Tank introduced me to pills, so I won't put it all on *Country*'s evil ass. It was how I could screw strangers in the beginning. After popping a Benzo or Zanny—*hmmmph!* I was ret to work. Gave me the buzz of alcohol, without the smell and burn. I know it don't make sense to you."

JoJo had learned enough about Roxi's druggie past for one day. "Have you seen, or heard from him?"

"Not at all."

"That punk's still on my list."

Good riddance thought Roxi. She didn't say it, but his days were numbered.

After what he did to me — arivederci! He won't beat on anyone else.

She knew, telling Keefy would set off a chain of events. He looked at her neck, and clenched his fist. "*I'ma see him.*"

He'd been upfront about his views on her choices, and inability to "*wife*" her. This drove her crazy, but his reaction to her plight, excited her. *For now — it's enough!*

Where he lived, his friends, and the type of car he pushed, were mysteries. She wanted to know more, but truthfully, it was insignificant. She didn't prod, or impose. Having him as a lover, satisfied more, than nothing.

The missing checkbook, could wait until she cleared her head. In the short-term, she needed an escape. "You feel like walking me to the bar?"

"Hell yeah! I'll check on Chanel, then we're outty."

"All right."

Once alone, an urge to sob came over her again. She gnawed her knuckle, longing for a sting, she could explain. Rohan was gone, and Kitty upped the ante.

"*Ya boy's gonna get his,*" replayed in her brain.

She has to know! Word has surely reached the gutter by now.

Nine times out of ten, that's where it started.

This cockeyed bitch probably thinks this ends with Chanel being assaulted.

JoJo wasn't a gangster, but somethings can't go unchecked.

37

DA BING

THREE MONTHS LATER

Based on the advice of other inmates, JoJo chose a bench trial.

"Your best hope is a judge who believes in redemption."

After observing the State's first witness, and her defender's incompetence during cross-examination, she took the prosecutor's deal. She pled guilty to battery, and received a twenty-month sentence. The Judge told her, *"You know better. You should've done better. If you abide by the rules, with the credit for time served, you can be home in less than a year. Good luck!"*

In her case, it being a *"first offense,"* made no difference.

"Maryland doesn't hand out time like they do in DC." They lied.

For weeks, she considered asking her grandparents to intercede. They had the type of connections she needed.

She could picture Merle's nose in the air, and her Giuseppe's clicking, as she stormed the courthouses' stairs. A faint trace of mint and rose in tow. She'd swoop in, and *"clean up the mess,"* to make herself feel like a hero.

"Your ways will land you in jail, one day, and those bull daggers with eat you alive. No pun intended!"

While awaiting her hearing, she analyzed the fateful day, and always reached the same conclusion—Life is a cruel instructor.

She gives you the test, then teaches you the lesson.

Roxi convinced her to switch to her drink of choice.

"It's less expensive and will get you just as bent."

"Cool." As long as it was *"dark,"* she was still honoring her friend.

She shouted at the man behind the Plexiglas wall. *"Eh, Habib! Give me a fifth of Paul!"*

"Is that his name?"

"Who knows? That's what he looks like to me."

"Girl—you's a fool! Ignorant as hell."

She remembered it being the first time, she'd smiled that day.

Why she assumed she could hang, with a functioning alcoholic, she'd never know. As the day waned, she craved a target for her vengeance. Roxi talked mad shit, so she dragged her along. The *"juice"* had her ready to snap a bitch's head off.

They found Kitty at a bar on Guilford Avenue, near the courthouse. It was the third they'd entered, but they would've searched all night. Simone stood at the counter, fawning over a balding city solicitor. Kitty and another *bird*, occupied adjacent stools. *"JoJo can get it too!"* followed by laughter and high fives, set her off.

Without speaking, JoJo dragged Kitty to the floor. Her Timberland boot, repeatedly connected, with the redbone's skull.

When her flunkies intervened, Roxi beat them back with haymakers and jabs. Dressed to brawl, she rumbled with the unprepared pair, until the owner sounded the alarm.

Terrified patrons flagged down a passing patrolman. He called for backup, and told the crowd to disband. Despite Roxi's pleas to flee, JoJo continued inflicting pain.

Hearing *"I'm gonna taze your black ass!"* brought her back to reality. Surrounded by angry faces, she threw her hands in the air. After it was over, she felt nothing, but shame.

As a sheriff tightened the cuffs, JoJo thought about Rohan.
"Never lose your cool. Instead of looking strong, you end up the fool."
Given her current predicament, his words were poignant.
He would be so disappointed.

During the ride back to the jail, she chastised herself for not listening. Months later, his death hurt like it just happened.

His funeral fell on a gray morning. Chanel sent flowers and signed *"Joanna Pierre"* in the guestbook. *"They sent him home like a king. Thousands of flowers, full choir, horse drawn carriage with a rider, silver casket, and the pall bearers, wearing white."* Per all reports, his wake was well-attended, but she hated second hand information.

She woke up early, and spoke through the window grate towards the sky. She thanked Rohan for the kindness, and revealed how much she loved him. A raven appeared out of nowhere. She imagined it carrying the dispatch into the heavens.

Though special, the tribute gave her little comfort.

While waiting her turn to exit the van, she knew nothing would ever be the same. JoJo hadn't prayed in years, but she asked God to send her an angel, or at a minimum, *keep me safe*.

To be continued.

NEXT UP

JoJo: Part Two

Lead Babies

ABOUT THE AUTHOR

Courtney "C-LOVE" Wheeler, born and raised in West Baltimore, MD USA, is a B-girl and lifelong story teller. She has an obsession with art of the African diaspora and dreams of creating work that illuminates the innate strengths and indelible weaknesses of humanity. Her interests include: Deviant behavior, Religion, Criminology, Mother/Daughter Relationships, Women in Hip Hop, S.T.E.M. Careers, Diversity, and Community Inclusion.

FOLLOW ME
Twitter: @clove410 | Instagram:@Clove410
Like my Author page
Facebook.com/AuthorCLOVE

If you enjoy this work, please leave a review:
goodreads.com/clove and amazon.com.

Paperbacks and e-books are available at
www.amazon.com/courtneywheeler and iTunes.